STRANGER
AT BAY

By the same author:

Of Things Not Seen

STRANGER AT BAY

DON AKER

Stoddart Kids

*We acknowledge the Canada Council for the Arts
and the Ontario Arts Council for their support
of our publishing program.*

A GEMINI YOUNG ADULT

Published in 1997 by Stoddart Kids,
a division of Stoddart Publishing Co. Limited
34 Lesmill Road
Toronto, Canada M3B 2T6
Tel: (416) 445-3333 Fax: (416) 445-5967
e-mail Customer.Service@ccmailgw.genpub.com

Published in the United States in 1998 by Stoddart Kids
85 River Rock Drive, Suite 202
Buffalo, New York 14207
Toll free 1-800-805-1083
e-mail gdsinc@genpub.com

Canadian Cataloguing in Publication Data

Aker, Don 1955-
Stranger at bay
"Gemini young adult."
ISBN: 0-7736-7468-3

I. Title.
PS8551. K46S77 1997   jC813'.54   C97-930671-X
PZ7.A3St   1997

Cover and text design: Tannice Goddard
Cover illustration: Albert Slark

Printed and bound in Canada

For my wife and daughters,
who still forgive me when I say,
"Just five more minutes."

Prologue

It's happening again. He can feel it coming. Like the thick wedge of sensation before a headache, forcing its way inside, making room where there shouldn't be any.

He rolls over, but he can't stop it. The sounds begin again like always, rising from nowhere. At first they're echoes of tiny hammers, staccato tapping on distant nails. Then they're the clatter of typewriter keys down a long hall, then the hard rap of knuckles on a nearby door. And then, finally, they're footsteps. Footsteps that frighten him. That have always frightened him, there behind the high green wall.

He moans softly, his eyes quivering behind sealed lids. He's searching for something, but all he sees is the green. It's all around him. Like he's fallen into a deep green well that's slowly filling with sound.

But it's not a well. Even through his fear he understands this. A well is a room in the earth. This isn't a room. Rooms don't move. Not like this green he's inside, that's inside him. The green carries him downward, pushing its way through dark layers that crack and heave before they shatter, sending dagger-like shards through the green and his brain.

His mouth opens in a sudden soundless scream.

Chapter 1

"Sure you got everything?"

I try not to sigh. I really do. But *got* should rhyme with *not* instead of *nut*, and I have to push back images of me roaming the countryside with a machete, ripping the bowels out of everything in sight. "Yes," I reply as I reach for the backpack between my feet.

If she heard the sigh, she doesn't let on. It appears she is serious about continuing the cease-fire that has existed in our household the past two days. "I packed you somethin' special for lunch," she says as I open the car door.

Something! Something special! I want to shout at her but, since she's looking at my back, I allow myself the silent luxury of one long roll of the eyeballs. Something I can't get away with at home now that my father has put his foot down. *Home.* Right. Like *this* could ever be *home.*

I get out and turn. "Thanks, Norma." I shut the door.

"Randolph?" My knuckles whiten on the door-frame. Her revenge: she knows how I hate that name.

I bend down to look through the window. Surprisingly, her face reveals no trace of the mockery I expect to see there. She's very good. Sometimes I have to remind myself of that.

"Yes?"

She brushes a lock of hair away from her eyes. Autumn Auburn — one of the eight or nine colors she prefers. I've never known her when her hair wasn't dyed, and I couldn't even begin to guess what her *real* hair color is. Probably mouse. With lots of gray mixed in.

"You sure you don't want me to go in with you?"

Yes. I'm dying to have my stepmother make me look like a two-year-old. "I'm sure."

"Well, take care then." She parts her lips in what I am supposed to believe is an encouraging smile. "Have a good day."

Like a frigging poster. All that's missing is the big yellow happy-face.

"You too, Norma," I say, allowing only a trace of sarcasm to seep through, then straighten and step back from the car.

The Lumina pulls away, and I'm left standing in front of an ugly brick building that looks a lot like the penitentiary we saw when we drove through Kingston, Ontario, on the way to Nova Scotia. A far cry from Eaton Academy. Two far cries.

I shoulder my backpack, trying not to think about the "somethin' special" Norma might have packed inside my lunch bag. Probably a Mr. Big chocolate bar. She knows how chocolate makes my face break out. Since turning fourteen last January, I've spent as much money on pimple cream as she has on hair dye. With equally attractive results. On a good day, my forehead looks like a slab of pepperoni. Which is why I wear my hair long in front.

Moving up the walkway toward the front entrance, I glance around me. The usual First Day Of School commotion: cars and buses vying for the right of way, teenagers shouting greetings at each other across the yard, garbled announcements spewing from an outdoor speaker mounted somewhere overhead. I hear something that sounds like *Wilbur cherry bacon peas retort domain surplus* and wonder what the person holding the microphone could have intended. Not that I think it's important, since no-one around me pays it any attention. It's just that words are kind of a hobby of mine. Sounds weird, I know, but I started talking in complete sentences when I was seventeen months old. My dad told me I'd never said a single word prior to that, and he and my mother — my *real* mother — had begun to worry that there was something wrong with me. More than likely, I just didn't have anything I wanted to say.

Wilbur cherry bacon peas retort domain surplus? I turn the possibilities over in my mind and come up with *Will Marjorie Baker please report to the main office.* Or maybe *Burt Orpington.* Or *Bill and Terry Beacon.* That's the trouble with being a New Kid. No frame of reference for translating Intercom Office-Speak.

I look around at all the people who obviously are not New Kids, envying them their easy confidence with each other and their surroundings. A handful of seniors stands on the edge of the street smoking, bursts of talk and laughter punctuating their hand-to-mouth movements. A larger group sits under a huge maple tree watching four guys with shaved heads kick a hackey-sack back and forth. Three girls lie on their backs on what masquerades as grass, their tank-tops pulled up over their flat bellies, showing earth-brown tans. All around them, kids walk up and down, up and down as if hoping to prove Einstein's theory that time for moving bodies slows down. As if they can delay the bell that will soon begin yet another school year. I know how they feel.

Actually, I feel lousy, and not just because it's my first day at a new school. I didn't sleep much last night. Nightmare, I guess, although I don't remember what it was about. I woke up around two o'clock, my heart hammering, my skin wet with sweat — a lot like the nights when I was little, after my mother left. Anyway, I spent the next couple of hours trying to convince myself I was still in Scarborough. Fat chance. The sofabed at our motel could double as tank armor, and the compressor in our kitchenette fridge sounded like an outboard motor at full throttle. By four o'clock I gave in and got up. Which explains the raccoon circles around my eyes. I suddenly wish my hair were even longer.

Stifling a yawn, I climb the front steps slowly, concentrating on where I'm putting my feet so I don't trip and make a fool of myself. I'm not good with stairs, especially in new surroundings. When I'm walking where people can see me coming, I get really self-conscious. I hate the way I walk. I mean, I put one foot in front of the other pretty much like everyone else, but the minute I think someone's watching me, my joints seize up and my body telegraphs an unmistakable *DORK ALERT!* to anyone within sight. I'd give anything to master that slow, rolling gait that lets everyone know you're cool. Whenever I try it, though, something happens to my hips and I look like one of those wind-up toys that tip over after three steps.

Fish says I think too much about it, that I need to forget what my feet are doing and just glide along. The problem is, when I forget about my feet they get the rest of me into trouble. Especially climbing stairs. For me, steps are booby traps, and I'm the Class-A Booby they lie in wait for. My first day at Eaton Academy two Septembers ago, I fell down an entire flight — from the very top to the very bottom. That's how I met Fish. He helped me hobble to a washroom where I hid till the halls were clear. I wish he were here with me now.

Once inside the school, I realize my earlier comparison to the Kingston Penitentiary was unfair. To the penitentiary. Everything here is gray. Walls, woodwork, lockers, even floors are done in shades of Early Battleship. The ceilings are the only exception. They, at least, are white, but their color only reflects and intensifies the grayness that reaches up to them. I feel like I've been swallowed by a brain whose life support was shut off a long time ago.

A sign reading MAIN OFFICE directs me toward a glass door that opens into a large room filled with people. An L-shaped counter separates a waiting area from a secretary's desk, beyond which are copying machines and doors leading to smaller rooms — behavior modification cells, as Fish would call them. I join the end of a line and practice my breathing.

Breathing is like walking. Too many people take it for granted, like all you need is a diaphragm and a pulse and the rest will take care of itself. When I'm nervous I breathe too fast, taking rapid shallow breaths, almost like a dog on a hot day. Marcia Hockstetter was kind enough to bring that little detail to my attention on the occasion of my first honest-to-goodness date.

I'd taken Marcia to our school dance and the DJ had put on that godawful "Stairway to Heaven" that's almost as old as my stepmother. I spent the first minute or two trying to find a rhythm, then gave up and just concentrated on not stepping on Marcia's feet and not tripping over my own. Halfway through it, Marcia looks up at me with her blue eyes wide, and I think, *This is it! The kiss! Don't blow it!* Her lips part and just as I'm about to lay one on her she says, "Do you know you're panting?" Quite the cold shower, that Marcia.

The line moves ahead slightly, as a kid who can barely see over the counter, thanks the secretary and leaves. I watch him go out, amazed that anyone that short can even feed himself, let alone attend high school. At Brookdale High, grades seven to twelve are all in the same building. Eaton Academy groups students in separate units according to age, ability, and interest. A grade nine student like myself would rarely see someone in grade seven, like Counter-Kid there.

A wave of homesickness suddenly crowds my throat. I really miss Eaton. Not to mention Fish and Booker and the Invention Convention and everything associated with it. For the millionth time I try not to resent my father for bringing us here. I force myself to breathe slowly, smoothly. Inhale. Exhale. Inhale. Exhale.

A bell — or, more accurately, an electronic whine — shrills over the PA and suddenly I'm a line of one as everyone in front of me grumbles and turns to leave. I look at my watch — 8:50. Norma told me school didn't start until nine o'clock. Watching the halls fill with people heading toward homerooms or the gym or wherever kids go on The First Day, I imagine what it will be like to walk into my own classroom. Not only do I get to be The New Kid, I get to be The New Kid Who Arrives Late. Norma's probably laughing her head off this very moment. Norma one, Randy nothing. I'll kill her.

"May I help you?"

I turn and face a middle-aged woman who has had one too many make-overs. With lips as bright as polished apples and cheeks layered with powder the color of cinnamon, her face looks like one of those frozen pies you microwave right in the box. I try not to stare.

"I'd like to register."

"You would, would you?" It's not so much a question as a comment, and she stands there watching me.

"Yes, I would." I'm not sure what else to say. Is there a secret handshake? Do I slip her money under the counter? I hear myself beginning to pant and I force myself to breathe more slowly.

She continues to look at me, and I suddenly get the weird impression she can see me without my clothes on. I take my backpack off my shoulder and hold it in front of me, rummaging through it for the papers I've brought with me from Ontario. When I find them, I place them on the counter. I leave the backpack where it is.

She sifts through them, her eyes quickly scanning several school documents, including letters of introduction from my curriculum advisor and Eaton's assessment officer, copies of each of last year's term reports, and a number the school can phone to request faxes of my most recent psychological and academic profiles.

"My, my," she says when she looks up again. She boxes the papers between her hands, aligning their edges perfectly, then returns them to me. "Very nice."

I stare at her. *Very nice?* "Don't you need these?"

"Not without a completed admissions form."

"Where do I get that?"

"From Mr. Martin."

"Who's Mr. Martin?"

"Our junior high guidance counsellor. He's the person in charge of registration and placement. You come here *after* you've seen him."

I look at her, slack-jawed. "You mean I've

waited here for over ten minutes and I'm not even supposed to *be* here?"

She leans toward me, reaching across the counter. I recoil, then realize she's pointing at a sign taped at groin-level in front of me: ALL NEW STUDENTS REGISTER AT THE GUIDANCE OFFICE, ROOM 108.

"You *can* read, can't you?" Her apple lips part in a parody of a smile.

I flush, jamming the papers into my backpack. "I read what I can *see*," I mutter. I want to suggest another place for her sign, but it wouldn't be any easier to see there, either. "Where's room 108?"

"Four doors down on your right. Remember, you're looking for Mr. Martin." She says this last part slowly, like I'm three years old.

I don't bother to thank her — I'm too busy trying to remember if Norma was abandoned as a child. I think I've found her mother.

Chapter 2

"Mr. Martin?"

A balding man in his mid-forties looks up from an explosion of paper that litters a gray metal desk. "Mmm?"

"I'm a new student. The office sent me here to register."

He gets up and comes around toward me, his hand extended. I offer him mine to shake but, instead, he walks right by it and opens one of several metal drawers that line one wall of his tiny inner office. Rummaging through file folders, he pulls out a long sheet of paper and hands it to me.

"You can take a seat out there and complete this."

Warm guy. Probably the secretary's brother.

"Out there" is an afterthought of a room that

separates his office from the hallway. Not much bigger than a bathroom, it contains three chairs, a small table, and a million pamphlets and brochures stuffed into wire racks screwed to the walls. I reach into my backpack for a pen, then take a seat and begin filling in the minuscule blanks and boxes. Street address (I'm not sure), phone number (we don't have one yet), the number of brothers and sisters living at home (none), and so on. The only important information I'm able to enter is my father's full name (Ronald Alexander Forsythe) and my previous school. I don't bother recording Norma's name; her blank is labelled MOTHER and there's not enough room to add STEP in front of it without writing over into my father's box. I'm not sure if I should write my real mother's name since she's been out of the picture for so long, so I don't write anything.

Before I finish, a girl about my age comes in and crosses to the doorway of the inner office. "Mr. Martin?" She speaks softly, her words like balls of cotton colliding with those rack-covered walls.

"Natalie!" I can hear the guidance counsellor getting up and coming around his desk. "It's so nice to see you! Did you have a good summer?"

I'm astonished. The man has a personality.

"Yes, I did." She seems embarrassed, speaking even more softly than before. I find myself straining to hear her.

"What can I do for you this morning, Natalie?" He's standing in the doorway now, beaming.

"Mrs. Holt ran out of 9-R timetables and asked me to get some extras from you."

"Those grade nine classes are bigger than we'd predicted." He turns and I hear him pulling out another file drawer. "Actually, we've had a big influx of students at almost every level. I've had a dozen more transfers since Friday, and more students are registering today."

Natalie looks in my direction. I, of course, am "More Students." I smile despite my obvious singularity. She smiles back and once again I have to remind myself to breathe slowly. She's pretty. Dark hair, fair skin. With serious eyebrows.

I'm a sucker for real eyebrows. It takes courage not to pluck them when every girl around you is yanking hairs out left, right, and center. Christine Ellsworth, a girl I knew at Eaton, shaved hers off completely last year and went around for months with this continual look of astonishment on her face. I don't think they ever fully grew back.

"Here they are." Mr. Martin reappears with a sheaf of papers. "These should be enough. If they aren't, tell Mrs. Holt to leave a note in my box and I'll run some more off when I get a chance."

"Thanks, Mr. Martin." She turns and leaves.

"Finished yet?"

I hear the question but it seems to be coming

from some place far away. It doesn't concern me. All I can do is inhale. I'm sitting in the wake of this incredible perfume, having forgotten that girls can smell so good. At Eaton you aren't allowed to wear perfume or cologne. Always sensitive to health issues, the school boasts a completely scent-free environment — that is, if you don't count the bathrooms after the cafeteria serves chili.

"If you've finished that form ..."

The guidance counsellor's voice trails off and I suddenly realize he's speaking to me. I swivel around. "Sorry. Yes, I've finished." I hand him the paper.

"Come in," he says, gesturing toward the inner room. "It's cramped, but it has a window."

I follow him inside and squeeze into a chair across from him. There is just enough space for my legs, although my knees bump against the front of his desk.

"Sorry I was so short with you before. I was trying to remember a name I'd forgotten." He holds up a scrap of paper. "Luckily, I wrote it down. Even luckier that I was able to find it in this mess," he adds, grinning. "Things are crazy here today."

I smile. He's human after all.

"I have some papers that my last school sent with me," I offer.

"Thanks, uh ..." He glances down at my registration form. "Randolph." He looks up. "Do you go by Randolph?"

I shake my head. "Randy."

"It's good to meet you, Randy. I'm Mike Martin, although you probably already know that or you wouldn't be here." He grins again. "You must have met the dragon lady."

"Dragon lady?"

"Mrs. Belcher. The school secretary. She likes to put students through the wringer, but she's really a sweetheart."

I stare at him blandly.

"No, really, she is. You just have to know what you want when you go into the office. She's a very busy woman. As long as you don't waste her time, she'll do whatever she can to help you."

I must look unconvinced because he changes the subject. "Where are those papers you said you brought?"

I pull them out of my backpack and pass them over.

"Mmm," he murmurs approvingly as he flips through them. "Eaton Academy. Fine school."

"You've heard of it?"

"I read about it in *Maclean's* magazine. The article called it one of the top five schools in Canada. And judging from these marks," he continues, "you certainly made the most of your time there."

I can feel my ears redden with embarrassment. "I have a good memory. It helps."

He scans another page, whistling softly. "Photographic?" he asks.

"Not really. I just have this weird knack for remembering what I've read. Something to do with the way my brain processes written language." I clear my throat, hoping he'll change the subject.

He does. Looking up, he asks, "What brought you to Nova Scotia, Randy?"

The Question. On our drive down from Ontario, I rehearsed a dozen different answers to it. I surprise myself by telling him the truth. "My dad lost his job."

He doesn't even blink. "Sorry to hear that." I expect him to ask me for more details, but he doesn't. He just sits there, his hands resting on the piles of papers in front of him, as if he's giving me time to say more if I want to. I suddenly want to.

"It's not like he got fired or anything. The company he works for is downsizing. 'Trying to do more with less,' is how they put it. My dad's job was phased out." I look at the mass of papers on his desk, so much like the piles of papers I was used to seeing in Dad's Scarborough office. "He had the choice of taking a severance package or transferring to another position. He took the transfer."

Mr. Martin looks at my registration form again. "I see your father works for Healthaid. What's that?"

"A pharmaceuticals firm."

"I don't think I've heard of it."

"They're just expanding into the Maritimes. Dad's now the sales rep for western Nova Scotia."

"I guess he'll be on the road a lot."

"Yes." No future tense required — he's on the road right now. That's why he isn't here with me today. Not that I'd want him to be; I'm certainly old enough to do this by myself. But it would have been nice to have had the option.

"No address or phone number?"

"We just got here the day before yesterday. We're staying at the Garden View Motel till we get moved in."

"Did your family buy a place here in town?"

I *wish*. "We have a house over in Lewis Cove."

His eyes widen. "You're on the bay, then. I'd have thought your father would want to be closer to the main highway since he'll be traveling so much. It can be tricky getting up over the North Mountain in the winter."

That had been one of *my* arguments, too, but it hadn't worked. "The house used to belong to my grandparents."

"Your father is from the Valley?"

I shake my head. "My grandfather was posted to the base in Greenwood for a year when my father was just a kid. I guess that's not far from here."

Mr. Martin nods. "Matter of fact, quite a few of

the kids here have families who work on the base."

"Grandpa was an electronics technician, but he thought he'd try his hand at farming in his spare time. He wasn't very good at it, and the place wasn't much to begin with. When he was posted out he didn't even try to sell it." I look out the window, embarrassed. "It's in pretty bad shape."

He smiles. "You'd be amazed at what a family can do with an old place, especially if any of you are at all handy."

I try not to laugh. The oven in our kitchenette wouldn't work last night when Norma was trying to cook supper, and she and Dad spent a good twenty minutes checking plugs and fuses. Frustrated, they finally called the owner, Fred Sampson. It took him all of eight seconds to discover that Norma had accidentally pushed in the timer button. Dad's administrative training and Norma's ability to find the home-shopping channel on any cable franchise don't exactly make them renovators *extraordinaire*. "I'd be *amazed* all right."

Mr. Martin must realize he's touched a nerve because he changes the subject again. "When do you hope to move in?"

"It depends on when the house is ready. Not for at least a week. Probably longer. There's a lot that needs to be done."

"No fun living out of suitcases, is it?"

I shake my head.

He smiles. "Well, at least we'll be able to get you settled into school faster than that." He twists in his chair and pulls out a file folder from a drawer marked Grade Nines. Opening it, he takes out several sheets of paper, each one bearing a list of names. "We have five grade nine classes at Brookdale —"

"Is there room for me in 9-R?" I blurt, surprising both of us.

He raises his eyebrows. "You know someone in 9-R?"

"Not really." I can feel the heat rising up the back of my neck. "I just thought . . ." What did I think? "The girl who was in here a few minutes ago . . ."

"Natalie McCormick?"

I nod. I don't want to have to say it. Luckily, he doesn't make me.

"Natalie's the daughter of a close friend of mine. A wonderful girl." He flips to the paper marked 9-R at the top, and I watch him add my name to the list below it. "She'd be an excellent person to help show you around and get you used to things."

He closes the folder and smiles. "Welcome to Brookdale High, Randy."

For the first time, I really do feel welcome.

Chapter 3

I try not to stare, but her desk is only one row over and one seat up from mine. Her hair falls over her shoulders in dark waves that remind me of the Bay of Fundy at night.

It's odd that I should suddenly think of the bay since I've only seen it once, the night before last when we arrived in Brookdale. As soon as we checked into the motel and had something to eat, Dad said he couldn't wait any longer, and he piled us back into the car. Like I really wanted to go. Even Norma, who is usually so accommodating of my father's wishes it makes me want to puke, complained she couldn't handle another minute in the Lumina. But Dad wouldn't take no for an answer and off we went to see "the old home-stead." He'd taken to calling it that on the drive down from Ontario. Like he'd lived there all his life instead of only one year, when he was seven.

I don't know what I expected. Having lived all my life in cities, I'd only seen farmhouses up close in pictures, and most of those were in magazines like *Country Living* and *Colonial Home* that Norma is forever picking up at supermarket check-outs. Maybe it was those pictures that conjured in my head an image of a white cottage with green shutters and a silver-blue pond glistening behind it. Whatever the reason, I certainly wasn't prepared for the abandoned hulk squatting at the end of a long, overgrown wagon-track my father called a driveway. A rambling one-and-a-half storey structure with a verandah sagging against the front, the house looked like it had undergone periods of mortar fire. *Heavy* mortar fire.

I had no idea what color it used to be since whatever paint it wore had long since peeled away leaving cracked and curling clapboards, weather-blackened and, in some places, rotten. Two of the windows were broken, a storm door hung at an acute angle over a rickety side step, and the roof dipped in the middle toward a chimney that looked to be missing as many bricks as it contained. Instead of a pond behind the house, a rock foundation and the remains of charred timbers marked where a barn had once stood. A Kodak Moment if ever I saw one.

"Isn't she great?" Dad breathed.

Great? I turned to make sure he was looking in the same direction *I* was. Amazingly, he was, his face like Christmas and Canada Day all rolled into one.

"Ron?" Norma was staring at the house the way I've seen people stare at highway accidents, and her voice had the same quaver in it I'd heard last Thanksgiving when Dad first brought her home to meet me. As appalled as I was by the derelict looming in front of us, I suddenly thought I might enjoy this.

"Mmm." Dad's eyes were shining and, for a moment, he reminded me of Jack Nicholson in that Stephen King movie. The one where the guy is possessed by evil spirits inhabiting an isolated hotel up in the mountains. Looking at "the old homestead," however, I knew no self-respecting evil spirit would come within a mile of the place.

"Did you realize it would be in this..." Norma hesitated a moment, then tentatively offered, "condition?"

Dad turned to us. "Oh, I know it doesn't look like much now, but we'll change all that. A couple of new windows, some paint, a little elbow grease and she'll be as good as ever. *Better* than ever, in fact."

Norma looked dubious, and I didn't blame her. Windows and paint aside, elbow grease just wouldn't cut it. We're talking grease from several major body parts here. Arm, shoulder, backbone, pretty much the whole torso. And throw in the legs and feet, too. Even then I doubted we could do more than elevate the place from cataclysm to catastrophe.

Dad opened the car door and got out. "C'mon, you two. I'll give you the ten-cent tour."

Norma and I followed like we were crossing a mine field, careful where we put our feet. Looking at the way her eyes scanned the tall grass, I could tell Norma was thinking about snakes. So was I.

Dad was already on the verandah shoving a key into a rusted lock. "Watch out for some of these floorboards," he warned, pointing at his feet. "A few need to be replaced."

Looking down, I thought it more likely that a few *didn't* need to be replaced. But I kept that observation to myself.

It wasn't so much the *sight* that greeted us that was so bad. Although the broken windows had let in some weather over the years, the roof of the verandah had kept out most of the rain and snow. There were a couple of dark ovals on the old wood floors where moisture had stained them, and dried leaves dotted the thick carpet of dust that lay everywhere, but the place didn't look as bad as I expected. The smell, on the other hand, was overpowering. Obviously, the house hadn't been *completely* uninhabited in the years since my grandparents had lived there. Those weren't raisins that speckled the floor and stuck to our shoes as we moved through the front hallway into what must have been the living room.

"This is the parlor," my father said.

Ha! I thought. Stick *funeral* in front of that and you've got the cover for *Better Tombs and Gravestones*. Although rays from the setting sun slanted through both windows, the room seemed to suck up the light like a shroud. Parlor, my foot.

Dad pointed at the stairway that ascended steeply along the far wall into a deepening gloom. "There are three bedrooms up there." He nodded ahead of him. "The kitchen's through this doorway. And, if I remember right, there's a dining room."

We shuffled after him like prisoners of war, careful not to brush up against the walls. I suddenly realized I was holding my breath. I exhaled, then began breathing through my mouth to avoid the smell.

The kitchen was obviously the largest room in the house. A huge wood-burning stove stood at one end by an enamel sink mounted below a window. A counter that looked about five feet long had open shelves above and below it. I didn't see any cupboards. I thought of the gleaming white Euro-designed cabinets we'd left behind in Scarborough, and I almost felt sorry for Norma. Almost.

Through a door on the left was a smaller room that must have been the dining room, but I didn't even want to *think* about eating. Not in *that* place.

I crossed the kitchen toward a door on the back wall. "What's this?"

"This," Dad said, opening it with a flourish, "is the bathroom."

Norma and I peered inside. At one time, the room probably had been a closet or pantry. Since then, someone had mounted a tiny window high in one corner and added a small white sink, a pink toilet, and a mauve tub. Dark brown stains circled the tub's drain and stretched up all four sides. There was no shower.

I felt my skin crawl. "I hope the upstairs bathroom is better than this."

"There *is* no upstairs bathroom," my father said.

I looked at him. "You're kidding."

He smiled. "Not yet, anyway. That'll come later."

"Later." It was the first time Norma had spoken since we'd entered the house and I could still hear the quaver in her voice. I smiled in spite of the bathroom.

Dad turned to her. "We'll make a list. *Two* lists. First, the top-priority stuff like the doors and windows. The roof and chimney, too. And paint. Once we get that done, we can start thinking about some of the other projects we'd like to tackle."

Tackle. Not once had I ever heard my father use the word *tackle*. He'd always been the sort of person who *undertook* projects, *launched* projects, even *instituted* projects. He'd never *tackled* a project in his life. I suddenly felt like I was trapped inside that PBS program, "This Old House." I half-expected to turn around and see Norm Abrams carrying in plywood or wallboard.

"When do you expect to do all this?" Norma asked.

Dad turned to look at her. "We'll *all* do it. Together. It'll be a family project."

My jaw dropped. "You're expecting *us* to get this place livable? In *my* lifetime?"

He shot me a glance and I could tell he was suddenly annoyed — when things don't go Dad's way, his nostrils flare big-time. But he kept his tone light as he explained, "I know it won't be easy, especially with me on the road so much, but we can get the place in shape if we all pitch in. It'll take quite a while just to get the inside cleaned up and aired out, and while we're doing that I'll hire someone to work on the outside. The roof and chimney come first, of course, along with the broken door and windows. Once we get settled in, we'll plan what it is we want to do next. Like fixing the verandah and painting everything. It'll be fun. You'll see."

"Yeah. Like it was going to be fun moving to Nova Scotia."

Dad's nose looked like it was about to sprout wings. "Randy, we've been all through this. I know you didn't want to leave your school and your friends, but I didn't have a choice. *We* didn't have a choice."

"I could have stayed with Fish and his parents. They offered —"

"I *know* what they offered. And it was certainly kind of them to extend the invitation. But I want you with me." He looked at Norma. "With *us*."

The One-Big-Happy-Family routine. "Yeah, right," I muttered, rolling my eyes.

I wasn't prepared for the explosion that followed.

"Now cut that out! I'm sick to death of your superior attitude, Randy. Whether you like it or not, Norma is family. *Your* family. So you can cut the holier-than-thou crap and finally accept the fact that she's a permanent part of the picture. From now on, you'll show her the respect she deserves. Do you hear me?"

I stared at him.

"And if I have to speak to you about this again, you can just forget about that Internet hookup you've been begging me for." He leaned toward me, his face inches from mine, and he put commas between each of his next five words. "Do I make myself clear?"

Ouch. No Net meant no online time with Fish and Booker. I nodded. Grudgingly.

He seemed satisfied. "Look," he continued, "I

know this place needs a lot of work. And, yes, things are going to be different here than they were in Ontario. But different doesn't mean worse. In this day and age, things change all the time, sometimes faster than we can keep up with them. Here's a chance for us to build some permanence into our lives, put down some solid roots. Together."

Roots. Hearing him say that word made me oddly uneasy. Not that it should, however. Dad and I had never grown anything before, not so much as a flower garden. We didn't even have plants in the house in Scarborough. Suddenly, though, I wondered why we didn't. A guy thing, maybe. Not having time to look after them. But, standing there in that excuse for a kitchen, I somehow doubted that was the reason. I didn't know why. Or even if I should think it was important.

Mistaking my silence for acquiescence, Norma gushed, "Well, if you guys are game, count me in, too. It'll be an adventure."

Dad put his arms around both of us. "Now *that's* the spirit."

We could have been posing for a beer commercial — the only thing missing was theme music. I stifled the urge to laugh, focusing instead on the window and the dark expanse that lay beyond the fields behind the house. The sun was bleeding on the horizon, large streaks of red staining the sky and the water separating us from New Brunswick. Even from this distance, I could hear the surge and crash of the waves against the cliffs where field dropped away to rocky shoreline.

Later, we drove the long way back to the motel, following the road that snaked along the bay before turning up over the mountain and back down into the Annapolis Valley. At times the car came within a house-length of the water and, disgusted as I was at the thought of moving into that derelict we'd seen, I watched mesmerized as black waves curled and crested, moving inexorably toward the rocks that destroyed them. Living in Ontario, I'd never seen the ocean except in movies. And even if this was only an arm of the Atlantic wedged between two provinces, I could still sense the power in it, could feel something magnetic in the way it held my gaze.

Much like the way I feel now watching Natalie McCormick. I know I should be listening to the teacher who's in the middle of this long explanation about course topics and evaluation procedures, but it's the sort of stuff everybody's heard before. He couldn't have made it more boring if he'd tried. He even has overheads of the handouts he's already given us, and we're supposed to be following along on the screen as he reads aloud. Jeez.

Mr. Martin brought me to this classroom after taking me to the dragon lady again. Although I still failed to see the "sweetheart" the guidance counsellor spoke about, Mrs. Belcher wasn't so bad when you knew what you were doing. Unlike the joker at the front of the room now. Mr. Hensford. He appears to have made time-wasting his life's work. We could have been through his Introduction To Grade Nine Maritime Studies fifteen minutes ago. I can only imagine how deadly the actual course is going to be.

"...and if you have any questions, I'll be happy to entertain them now."

Great. He doesn't answer questions, he *entertains* them. Quite possibly by putting them to sleep first.

Hey, maybe I'm on to something here. *Student Discovers Alternative Anaesthetic! Doctors Astonished as Teacher Sedates Patients! Randy Forsythe Wins Nobel Prize for Medical Breakthrough!*

The PA suddenly whines, catching Mr. Hensford in mid-sentence and me in mid-yawn. "Make sure you read the rest of your handouts this evening. I'll pass out your textbooks tomorrow. See you then."

We all shuffle to our feet and head for the door. Natalie turns to me. "What's next on your timetable?"

When Mr. Martin brought me to Hensford's room, he introduced me to the class, then asked Natalie if she'd mind showing me around the rest of the day. She didn't. At least, she said she didn't. And a girl with hair like that wouldn't lie, would she?

I glance down at the paper Mr. Martin gave me, mentally thanking the guidance counsellor again for putting me in 9-R. "Music."

"Not art?"

"No. Why?"

"The class splits for music and art. You can't take both because they're scheduled at the same time."

"Which one are you in?"

"Music."

There *is* a God. "Where is it?"

"Follow me."

She leads me out into the hallway where hoards of kids are weaving past one another. I spy Counter-Kid, his head bobbing around people's waists as he darts in and out, before disappearing around a corner.

"The music room is on the first floor at the other end of the school," Natalie explains as she leads me up a set of stairs.

She moves like a dancer, and I try not to stare as she climbs three steps ahead of me. "If it's on the first floor, why are we going upstairs?"

She turns, her hair cascading over one shoulder. "Last year they renovated the whole school. The architect made a lot of changes."

"Changes?"

"New library, new science labs, stuff like that. The best thing, though, was converting the typing room into a computer lab. State of the art. The school's hooked up to the Net now."

She seems thrilled. So am I. "You surf?" I ask.

"I did before my brother, Barry, went to university. He was paying for the hookup. My parents said I could keep it if I paid for it, but it's a lot of money for something I can get for free at school. Seniors have priority, but I can be persistent if I really want something."

We reach the top of the stairs. "What about the music room?"

"Not all the school's changes make sense," she continues. "One of them is you can't get to the first floor music room without going upstairs, across to the west end of the school, and then down. Otherwise, you have to walk through the gymnasium. The gym teachers have a fit if you try that."

"Same architect choose the color scheme?" I ask, nodding toward the gray walls of the hallway we're walking along.

"Same one."

I stick my finger in my mouth and mime a gag. She smiles and my heart stops. The thing is, she seems completely unaware of how beautiful she is. I rack my brain trying to remember what we were talking about. "Uh, umm . . . How much did all these improvements cost?"

We come to another set of stairs and start

down. "Four million dollars. Maybe a little more."

I whistle. "I guess you only get what you pay for."

She smiles again and we are at the music room. We must be, because I hear bells and chimes like a gigantic calliope sounding inside my head. I can't stop grinning. I'm sure I look like an idiot, but I can't help it.

Chapter 4

"Randy, this is Sherlyn, Monica, and Jake. Guys, this is Randy Forsythe. He just moved here from Ontario."

Music class is over, and Natalie and I are sitting in the cafeteria facing a poster that says: *ON THE INTERNET, NO-ONE CAN HEAR YOU SCREAM*. The place is packed with teenagers and I've been dreading this moment: Meeting People While I'm Eating. I'm always sure I've got food on my face or between my teeth. I wonder if everyone is as paranoid as I am. "Hi," I say, nodding my head toward the people who pull up chairs and sit down across from us.

Both girls are blonde, but the resemblance doesn't end there. They must be sisters, maybe even twins, because they have the same face: oval-shaped, with an upturned nose, and golden skin dusted with freckles. They're taller than Natalie with long legs and arms, reminding me of the swimmers on Eaton's varsity team. Jake is tall, too, maybe six feet, and the tank-top he wears reveals hard knots of muscle in his shoulders and arms. His neck looks to be nearly as thick as my thigh.

He sticks his hand out and I shake it, hoping I don't have Miracle Whip on my palm. The "somethin' special" Norma packed in my lunch was a Miracle Whip sandwich. I'm crazy about the stuff. I can eat it with a spoon right out of the jar. And I do if there's no-one around. Norma must've picked up a bottle at a convenience store yesterday because everything else in town was closed for Labour Day. She probably spit on the bread when she buttered it, but it's good to be eating something normal again. I never thought I'd get tired of take-out.

Then Jake leans across the table and sticks a fork in my chest. Or he may as well have — he plants a big sloppy kiss on Natalie's lips. Then he says, "So, babe, what class are you in?"

Babe? She goes with someone who calls her *babe?*

Natalie reddens, glancing around to see if the woman at the cash register has seen. "9-R. With Randy."

Sherlyn unzips a lunchbag that would give a

knapsack an inferiority complex, and takes out an already-open bag of chips. Crunching into one, she says, "The three of us are in 9-W. I saw Kyle at recess and he said he's in 9-A."

"What about Phil and Erin?"

"9-B," Monica offers. "And poor Steve's in 9-S all by himself."

"The gang really got shuffled around, didn't they?" This from Jake who has just shoved half a chocolate bar into his mouth, and sounds like he's doing some heavy-duty shuffling in there himself. I wonder if he'll break out in zits like I would if I ate that, but somehow I know he won't. He has an air of invincibility about him that makes me doubt he even gets wet when it rains. I dislike him already.

Until now, I've had Natalie pretty much to myself. After music class came a fifteen-minute break that we spent at the office trying to sign out lockers. Unfortunately, about a hundred other kids had the same idea and our line-up never even got beyond the office entrance before the bell for third period rang. But I didn't mind — I'd have stood all day long on my head if it meant being inches away from Natalie McCormick of the long, wavy hair.

Our third and fourth classes were a double-period in the computer lab. And, although the year-old facility isn't as flashy as Eaton's computer department, the machines are plenty powerful. Best of all, the teacher, Mrs. Lloyd, didn't spend four years telling us what we already knew. In fact, she got us started on the computers almost immediately and encouraged us to goof around so she could get a sense of everyone's individual skill level.

Natalie and I logged onto the Net and entered a chat room where I asked and she answered all kinds of questions about Brookdale, the school, and herself. She wrote me quite a bit, mostly about her family, where she lived, what she liked to do — stuff like that. Unfortunately, she failed to mention Jake who, at this very moment, is in the lunch room with her, me, and the others.

"So, Randy, what brings you to Brookdale?" He's asking me the question, but he's looking at Natalie like she's on the menu right after the chocolate bar. And she's looking at him the same way.

I think I'd give just about anything to have her look at me that way. Beneath those incredible brows are eyes you could swim in. I know that sounds corny, something you'd hear in a low budget World War II flick where the love-struck pilot describes the woman in the French Underground who helped him cross enemy lines. But it's true. They're like deep pools. Or those dark stones in men's signet rings. Or —

Sherlyn is saying something. I turn to look at her. "Earth to Randy," she repeats.

I flush, imagining the *DORK ALERT!* hovering

over my head. I grin stupidly. "Yes?"

"Jake asked why you moved here."

"I murdered a guy."

I have absolutely no idea why I said that. It just popped out, like a chicken bone after the Heimlich maneuver. It certainly wasn't on the list of answers I'd practiced on the drive down from Ontario. But you can bet they're all looking at me now. Even Jake.

Natalie's eyes are enormous. "Randy Forsythe, you did not murder anyone."

The smart thing to do would be to wink or smile or chuckle or any of a dozen other things to end the joke. The *smart* thing. But I like the way she's looking at me now, and my mouth suddenly shifts into overdrive and I'm talking with no idea at all of what's coming next. "With these two hands."

What are you doing? I struggle to breathe normally, positive my face must be three shades of red. The Miracle Whip sandwich I'm holding suddenly feels like a facecloth, and I lay it on the waxed paper Norma wrapped it in.

"Yeah. Right." Jake looks at me like I'm something you'd wipe off a slide in a biology lab.

Monica and Sherlyn, on the other hand, seem fascinated. "Really?" Monica breathes. "You actually *killed* someone?"

I nod, trying to look bored with the whole topic. "He had it coming."

Sherlyn's mouth sags open, her potato chips

forgotten. "Who was it?"

"Someone I knew."

"A friend?"

"You could say that."

"What did he do?" Natalie asks, an undercurrent of awe in her voice.

"Do?" I ask. I'm stalling. I have no idea what to say next.

"Yeah," Jake snorts. "What's worth killin' a guy for?" Of course he doesn't really believe me, but I can tell part of him wants to. Part of *me* wants to. I've gone too far, but I don't know how to stop this without looking like a total jerk.

Then I see it. Right in front of me. My way out of this. "Absolute Access."

He arches his eyebrows. "Absolute *what?*"

Then Natalie is laughing. Monica, Sherlyn, and Jake look at her like she has two heads. "What's so funny?" Jake demands.

Natalie reaches across and puts her hand on his arm. "Jake, Randy's talking about a computer game. It's the latest thing on the Internet. Barry showed me how to log onto it when he was home this summer. I played it a few times but I always got killed." She looks at me, smiling. "You must be good."

I smile back, relieved. "Lucky is more like it."

Jake looks closely at the two of us, a scowl on his face, and suddenly I don't feel quite so lucky anymore.

* * * * * *

"So, what *did* bring you to Brookdale?" Jake asks.
He's sitting on the grass beside Natalie, one arm
draped over her shoulder. We're now nine, having
been joined on the soccer field by four other ninth-
graders. I'm not great with names — I usually
forget them if I meet more than two people at
once, because I'm concentrating more on trying
not to look like a geek than on the people I'm being
introduced to. But this time I tried something
Booker told me about: saying a name over and
over in my head while I focused on something
about the person that stood out. It worked. Kyle
Mosher: kinky black hair (like a floor mop plugged
into a light socket); Phil Gerrard: huge feet (at
least size fourteen); Erin Vessey: earrings everywhere (even her ears). Then there's Steve Carson.
Steve required absolutely zero imaging on my part
to insert into long-term memory. In fact, it would
be tough *not* to remember the name of the guy sitting up on the bleachers beside Monica. Actually,
sitting doesn't accurately describe their present
activity — if they were any closer they'd be sharing a vital organ. These two have been lip-locked
for the better part of five minutes, including the
few moments when Natalie first introduced me to
the guy. In the middle of what Booker would call
the tonsil tango, Steve poked his hand at me and
grunted something that sounded like a cross

between a greeting and a gargle. Very wet. I think I was supposed to be impressed, but he reminds me of a guy at Eaton that Fish once described as *bar-b-cubed*: blonde, blue-eyed, and bored with anything that didn't focus entirely on him. I get the feeling the lip-lock is Steve's way of letting me know (and reminding everyone else) who's *really* special around here.

I tell Jake about my dad's transfer. The others — with the exception of Steve and Monica — show polite interest, but I can sense Jake's boredom. He looks like he'd rather be tossing around a football than sitting here listening to me.

"I never heard a' Healthaid before," says Kyle. "Sounds like a kids' drink." The others chuckle and so do I.

"You're right, it does," I say. "Actually, they talked a lot last year about changing it."

"Cause it sounds like a drink?"

I shake my head. "Because of the *aid*. They thought a health care company shouldn't sound like a terminal disease."

"Health care?" Jake asks, and I can hear the sudden interest in his voice.

"You know, vitamins, antihistamines, drugs like that."

Above us, Steve pulls his face away from Monica's so abruptly their lips make a suction-cup sound. "Drugs?"

I glance up. Steve's mouth looks like mine

after I've eaten watermelon, all wet and shiny, but for the first time he's not looking at Monica. "Yeah," I say. "Quite a few."

"Any steroids?" Jake asks.

I'm surprised at his question, then note the size of his neck again. "I think so. But mostly they're into pain relievers."

"Why's that?" asks Natalie.

Jake looks at Natalie, his face like a footprint, the obscure track of something that's just passed over it. But I'm not sure what.

"That's where the big money is. Pain relief is the bread-and-butter of pharmaceuticals," I add, quoting a line my father always uses, then grimace at how ridiculous it sounds. "Especially cold remedies. Healthaid makes one of the best-selling analgesics in Canada." My God, I sound like a talking billboard. I want to change the subject but don't know how. Thankfully, Kyle does it for me.

"So your dad's a traveling salesman?"

I smile, relieved. "He prefers the title Regional Representative. But it pretty much comes down to traveling salesman."

Phil-with-the-feet shrugs. "I wish *my* old man was a traveling anything if it would get him away from the house."

The others laugh and Kyle lets me in on the joke. "Phil's dad got laid off from the tire plant in Waterville this spring so he started his own business."

Phil frowns. "You know those environmental depots the government set up to recycle drink containers?"

I nod.

"My dad got the contract for this end of the county."

"You make it sound like it's worse than being laid off."

"Stop by my place sometime 'n you'll see."

Erin elbows him in the ribs good-naturedly. "Phil isn't exactly Brookdale's Entrepreneur of the Year."

I smile at her humor but Phil does not. "I used t' have a room all to myself," he grumbles. "Now I share it with a zillion pop cans."

"The depot is in your house?"

He shakes his head. "In our garage. But last year I convinced my parents to let me fix up a room in the back."

"Phil has a set of drums," offers Natalie by way of explanation. I nod.

"I *wouldn't* have," Phil continues, "if I'd known *this* was goin' t' happen. Now all the overflow ends up there."

Jake suddenly pulls himself to his feet. "Speakin' a' overflow, I gotta take a leak."

"Me, too," says Phil.

It's like some weird kind of signal because all the guys are getting up, even Steve. I'm not sure what to do. Do I stay here and look stand-offish?

Or go with them and look like one of those pathetic hangers-on? Why hasn't someone come up with a rule book for times like this? *A Teenager's Guide for Awkward Moments*. Of course, if there *was* one, it'd probably be written by some middle-aged moron who can't even remember what it was like to *be* a teenager. Or by someone like Norma whose idea of social graces can be summed up in five words: *Just don't make a scene.*

I reach into my backpack and dig around like I'm looking for a winning lottery ticket because I don't know what else to do. Surprisingly, it's Jake who extends the invitation. "You comin', Randy? We only got a few minutes before the bell."

Thank you, thank you. I glance at Natalie. She's looking at Jake, but he's not looking at her.

"Sure," I say, getting to my feet and shouldering my backpack. "We have science next, don't we, Natalie?"

She turns to me, her mouth open as if about to tell me something. But she just nods.

"That'd be Connor's room," says Kyle. "106, just down from the guidance office. I'll show you where it is." I smile appreciatively at him, but he looks away.

"Thanks. See you there, Natalie," I say, then shamble off after the guys.

* * * * * *

"Wanna smoke?" Jake asks.

We're in a second-floor washroom with the windows wide open, Jake and Steve each sucking on a cigarette while Phil and Kyle stand by the door watching the hallway. Steve doesn't surprise me — he's obviously orally fixated, completely lost without something to occupy his mouth. Jake, on the other hand, looks like he'd be more careful about what he does to his body. Anyone into strength training (heck, anyone who watches TV) should know the harmful effects of smoking. Then again, even Arnold Schwarzenegger smokes cigars, doesn't he? Go figure.

I pull up my zipper and step away from the urinal. "No thanks." For the life of me, I don't know why they aren't doing this out on the sidewalk. Smoking on school property is punishable by an automatic three-day suspension. I know because it's in the student handbook Mr. Martin gave me. I read it during Maritime Studies when I wasn't looking at Natalie. Anything to avoid listening to Hensford drone on about his course outline. I don't smoke, anyway, but if I did I sure as hell wouldn't do it here and risk getting caught by a teacher on my first day at Brookdale High. How To Make An Indelible Impression. Cripes.

"So. Randy." Jake's two words hang there in the washroom like the blue smoke hovering over our heads.

Something seems to be happening here. I'm not

sure what it is, but the others appear to know. Phil looks down at the floor like he's suddenly fascinated by tile grout — dark gray, of course. Kyle continues to look out the door, but I get the impression it's not just because he's on teacher-watch. Something about the way he runs his hand through his hair, the same way Norma does when she's looking through a cookbook and finds words with more than two syllables: like she'd prefer to skip that part but knows she has to slog through it anyway.

Only Steve and Jake are looking at me. Steve is grinning. Jake is just standing there, his arms crossed, making the veins in his biceps look like coiled snakes. I swallow, and the sound in my throat seems to echo off the gray concrete walls around me.

"So. Jake." As nonchalant as the target of a firing squad. Where's a good blindfold when you need one?

Jake sucks on his cigarette again, then drops it on the floor and leans toward me, his face inches from mine. "New guys gotta learn lotsa new rules," he says.

"Rules?"

"Yeah. Rules. About how things operate around here. And who does the operating."

And now I know what's coming, what this is all about. "Jake, about Natalie —"

But Jake is one of those people who like to say things for themselves. Spell it out. "Last guy who messed with Natalie ended up with a broken face."

Steve snorts. "More like a mashed face."

Jake leans even closer, and I can smell beneath the cigarette smoke the sour darkness of the chocolate bar he wolfed down earlier. My stomach twists and I suddenly know I'll never be able to eat anything chocolate again. "Understand what I'm tellin' you, Randy?"

I nod. "I understand, Jake."

Suddenly he reaches out and slaps me on the back, whooshing the air from my lungs. "I had you pegged as a quick learner right from the start." He smiles. Steve, on the other hand, seems disappointed. His grin is gone.

"Someone's comin', guys."

We all turn to Phil who jerks his head toward the hallway. "Not a teacher. Some kid."

I'm able to breathe again. Two close calls in ten seconds — Fish and Booker will hoot when they hear.

Footsteps approach and then we're all looking at Counter-Kid standing in the doorway, his right foot frozen in mid-step. He's got that *Wrong place, Wrong time* look on his face that I'm sure I must have been wearing only a moment ago. I look at Steve and see his grin is back.

"Bobby!" Steve breathes, the softness of his tone not masking the menace in his voice. "How's it hangin', man?"

Counter-Kid gulps. Literally. His right foot drops and he stands there looking like a cat about to spring. Backwards. I know how he feels.

"Hi," he says, his voice soft and high like a girl's. He flushes, clearing his throat. "Hi, guys." This time his voice is deeper, but I can hear beneath it a quaver. So can everyone else.

Steve moves toward him. "Private washroom, Bobby. Din't y'know that?"

Counter-Kid flushes again. "No. I didn't. Sorry." He takes a step backward.

Steve reaches out and puts a hand on Counter-Kid's shoulder. Steve is so much taller that, for a moment, he looks like a father towering over a son. But only for a moment. The illusion vanishes when Counter-Kid grimaces, and I can see the knuckles on Steve's hand whiten as he grips the kid's shoulder. "Don't rush off, Bobby. Sometimes we make exceptions." He turns to the rest of us, his grin even wider than before. "For a price, that is. Right, guys?"

"Absolutely," Jake says, smiling graciously. Kyle and Phil murmur in agreement. I, of course, stand there like an idiot, not knowing what's coming next.

Counter-Kid is all eyes. "A price?" he asks, his voice like thin glass about to break.

Steve throws his other arm around the kid's neck, leading him into the washroom.

"Yeah, we're an equal opportunity operation

here, Bobby," Steve coos. "It's just that equality costs. How much y'got?"

Now both Counter-Kid and I know the score. "Look, I can use another washroom." The kid tries to back away, but the arm around his neck tightens. Steve bends down, his face so close to the kid's their noses almost touch. "I asked you a question, Bobby," he breathes, his voice so low I can barely hear him. "How much y'got?"

Counter-Kid's voice is a strangled sob. "A couple of dollars."

Steve turns to the rest of us. "Whaddya think, guys? Is two bucks enough?"

Jake crosses his arms again and I watch Counter-Kid's face as the veins in Jake's biceps coil. "I dunno, Steve. Equality ain't cheap."

Steve nods knowingly. "I hear ya, man. But this bein' the first day 'n all, maybe we can have ourselves a sale." He grins. "A grand openin' sale, just for little Bobby here." He turns to the kid. "Looks like this is your lucky day, Bobby." He sticks out one hand, the other still clamped on the kid's shoulder. The kid's face is so red you'd swear every capillary in his cheeks has exploded. He sniffs, then reaches down into the left pocket of his jeans and pulls out a five dollar bill.

Steve's eyes widen. "Bobby, Bobby, Bobby," he sighs. "I'm goin' to assume you were a little confused a moment ago. Otherwise, I'd have t'think you lied to me about the two bucks." He leans closer. "I get upset when people lie to me. *Real* upset. Know what I mean?"

The kid sniffs again and I know he's about ten seconds from bawling. I feel like a jerk standing here watching this. Where the hell is a teacher when you need one? I'd even settle for Hensford, who probably has an overhead for even this occasion.

Steve lets go of the kid's shoulder and pockets the money. "We'll let it go *this* time, okay? But don't you *ever* try that again." He steps back and makes a grand sweeping gesture with his arm. "The washroom's all yours, Bobby."

Apparently, the kid's need to relieve isn't as great as his need to *leave*. He turns and is gone, his footsteps echoing down the empty corridor. I hear a door bang open and the footsteps fade into a stairwell as Jake and Steve high-five each other, then poke Phil and Kyle in the ribs. They, too, grin foolishly.

I think I'm going to be sick.

Chapter 5

"This is Connor's room here," Kyle says. "106." These are the only words he's spoken on our way here. I haven't said anything, just followed him when the bell rang shortly after Bobby, the Amazing Counter-Kid, disappeared.

"Thanks." I don't know what else to say. Or even if I *should* say anything else. Kyle isn't exactly the person I thought he was. None of them are. Not even Natalie. How can someone like her be mixed up with a bunch like this? Jeez. I turn to go in.

"Randy?"

I look back. "What?"

"Jake and Steve just like to have fun. We all do."

"I can see that." I don't mean for that to sound as sarcastic as it does, but it's out there before I can do anything about it.

He seems annoyed. "No harm done, okay?"

I'm not sure what he's referring to: Jake's threatening to rearrange my face or Steve's taking the kid's five bucks. Either way, it seems like a pretty stupid thing to say. He suddenly seems to think so, too, because he frowns, then nods for me to step back from the door. I do, allowing a bunch of other kids to stream into the classroom. Kyle moves to the other side of the hallway and I follow.

He turns to me. "Look, you seem like an okay guy. Natalie likes you, and that says a lot. For me, anyway." He grins and I get the Jake-joke, smiling in spite of how miserable I feel. He continues. "I don't know what things were like where you come from, but here you kinda *go* along to *get* along. Know what I mean?"

"I'm beginning to."

"Jake and Steve can do a *lot* for you, you know? They're pretty important guys. You'll see."

"Randy!"

We turn and see Natalie coming down the hall toward us. She seems relieved to see us. Now I know why.

Kyle lowers his voice. "Remember what I said, okay?" Then, louder, "He's all yours, Nat. Gotta run. I got Hensford this period." He rolls his eyes and then he's gone.

Natalie stops beside me. "Everything okay?"

"Couldn't be better," I say, then follow her into Mr. Connor's science class.

* * * * * *

My backpack feels like a lead weight as I trudge into the parking lot of the Garden View Motel. Every teacher except Hensford issued textbooks today, but for some reason the office has decided not to assign any more lockers for awhile. So we have to lug everything around till they do. By Friday, my shoulder should be an open, oozing sore. Which, of course, reminds me of Norma.

"Hello," I call when I get to our unit, the last one in a row of fourteen. The Lumina is parked outside and the inner door is wide open, probably to let cool air blow through, but the outer screen door is locked. Norma isn't comfortable unless there's a locked door between her and the world. Forget the fact that any two-year-old could put his fingers through the screen in less time than it would take my stepmother to spell *intruder*. I don't have a key for the screen door, so I bang on it. *"Norma!"*

"Shhhhh!"

The sound is so close to my ear I nearly leap out of my skin. Whirling around, I bump the nose of a girl standing behind me.

"Ow!" she yelps, holding onto her nose.

"Jeez!" I exclaim, mortified. I see she's dropped a paper bag so I reach down to retrieve it, standing up at exactly the same time she stoops down to get it. The side of my head connects squarely with her forehead, the sound like a brick hitting pavement.

"OW!" This time she clutches both her nose and her forehead, making her look like those SEE NO EVIL, SPEAK NO EVIL monkeys you find in novelty shops. With my hand holding the side of my head, I realize I probably look like the HEAR NO EVIL component of the trio. I sigh. *DORK ALERT! DORK ALERT!*

"Are you all right?"

She turns and I notice a thread-thin line of red coming from her right nostril. Just great.

"You're bleeding."

"Am I?"

I don't expect the question. Would I lie about something like that? "Uh, yeah. Not a lot. Just a little from your nose there." I point my finger just as she bends down to get the bag she's dropped a second time, and my finger goes right up her nostril.

Oh

my

God.

She shrieks. I stagger back, my finger still extended. This time, however, there's a large red blotch on the end of it, and when I look up I see her nose is really bleeding now, like I've poked a hole in a dam.

She sees my finger, too. "What have you *done?*" she hisses, cupping her hands over her nose. She looks like one of those Great Outdoors types about to let loose with a moose call. Or the mating honk of the trumpeter swan. She tentatively pulls her hands away from her face, and her fingers are covered with red. She moans, and I see her start to sway. "I feel sick . . ." she begins, and suddenly she's got her head down between her legs and I'm looking at her back and her bum.

I don't have the slightest idea what to do. It's like I've stepped into one of those old Carol Burnett sketches you still see sometimes on late-night cable. All we need is the laugh-track to complete the picture.

"Dar you juss goan do sdan dere?"

"Sorry?" I ask, still looking at her bum.

"I *said* dar you juss goan do *sdan* dere?"

Then I know what she's asking. "What do you want me to do?"

She sighs, the sound long and deep. And wet. Below her on the ground and her paper bag are several large red drops, and I suddenly realize she's losing a fair amount of blood. "For sdarders, you can ged be a Gleenex."

"You should really have your head up and back."

"Ged be a *Gleenex!*" she hisses.

I start to panic. I'm no good in emergency situations. I'm the last guy you'd want to have on the other end of your 911 call. Locked out of our unit, I have no idea where I can find a Kleenex or anything else for this girl to stick up her nose. Until, of course, I remember my backpack. Whenever Norma packs a lunch, she includes more napkins than food. It's as if she's afraid whatever she's packed will suddenly take on a life of its own and smear itself over the entire body of the person eating it. The Save-a-Tree people would freak if they knew about Norma and her napkin fetish. I reach into my backpack and rummage around, taking out a handful of the absorbent white squares and handing them to the girl.

She shoves the whole mass over her nose, then slowly stands up. "Ooo," she moans, still wobbly. I reach out and take her elbow to steady her, but she pulls back. She obviously wants no more help from me.

"I'm going to bend down to get your bag now," I say slowly, as though talking to a person who hasn't spoken English for a while. I reach down, nab the paper bag, then straighten up and pass it to her. "Here."

"Nnnngks."

"Is there anything else I can do?"

She shakes her head.

"You're sure?"

But she's already moving away, heading toward the small house that serves as both the office of the Garden View Motel and the home of the owners, Fred and Linda Sampson. Probably to report the psycho in Unit 14.

It's then that I realize I haven't even said I'm sorry.

"Hi, Randy."

I jump again. If this keeps up, I'll need a pacemaker by tomorrow. I turn and see Norma standing in the doorway. She unlatches the screen door and I go in.

"Where *were* you?" I ask, but I already know the answer. It doesn't take a sleuth to realize the significance of the bathrobe she's wearing. Or, for that matter, the towel on her head.

"In the shower. I just got back from cleaning the house all day. I was filthy." And, as if to underscore her words, she shudders. "I see you met Colleen."

"Colleen?" I ask, opening the tiny refrigerator in the kitchenette. I root around inside for something to eat and settle on an apple.

"The girl who just left. What happened to her?"

I shrug. "Long story. Who is she?"

"Daughter of the people who own this place. She helps out quite a bit. She stayed home from school today to give the couple in Unit 7 a break. They're from New Brunswick, traveling with a baby boy. They were up all night with him. Colic or something. I think all three of them are sleeping right now. Try not to make any noise when you go outside, okay?"

Norma and her news flashes. "Okay."

She goes into the bedroom and I hear her getting dressed. "How was school?"

I sigh. She's attempting her Successful Stepmother Asks About The Child's Day routine, which is Chapter 4 in her *Stepmother's Guide to Successful Parenting*. I found the book on her nightstand the week before we left Scarborough and read it for a laugh. Now, for the first time, I regret my ability to remember everything I've read — I'd give a lot to forget *that* drivel. "Fine," I say around a mouthful of apple. I slump onto the sofa that doubles as my bed at night.

"Meet anybody?"

That, of course, is the non-threatening means of determining whether I've made any friends. The Successful Stepmother isn't supposed to ask a question like that outright for fear of making The Stepchild feel inadequate in the event he *hasn't* made any friends. I can't believe someone actually got paid to write that garbage. I ignore her and pick up the remote control and flick on the TV. I may as well get my fill of shows now — I'm pretty sure Lewis Cove doesn't get cable.

Norma comes out wearing clean shorts and a t-shirt. "Don't get comfortable. You 'n me are goin' over to the house. I just came back to pick you up."

My back to her, I roll my eyes. "You and *I*. Nominative case, Norma."

She doesn't say anything for a moment. Then, "Whatever. C'mon. We got work to do."

"We *have* work to do," I say, my eyes on a "Price Is Right" contestant who has just given a ridiculously low estimate of the value of her prize showcase.

I, however, seldom underestimate Norma. I can usually tell exactly when she's about to blow. Which should be just . . . about . . . NOW.

"Randolph Forsythe, if you think I'm gonna stand here and play your stupid little grammar games, you got another think *comin'!*"

Bingo. I turn to face her, smiling innocently. "Remember, you don't want to wake those people in Unit 7."

I love stopping her in mid-explosion. She looks like a fish out of water, her mouth working but nothing coming out. Finally, she goes to the door and slips on her sneakers. "There's lots to be done over there, and since there's no electricity yet, we only got . . ." She pauses, her lips a thin line, then continues, "We only *have* until the light runs out. It's a lotta work, 'n you sittin' on that sofa's not gonna get the job done." Her chin out and her head high, she glares at me. "Now get in the car."

It's quite the little speech. I have to dock her, of course, for diction, and she needs to work on poise and presentation, but the whole assertiveness thing works for me. A solid eight out of ten. Maybe even eight-and-a-half.

I pull myself up and click off the TV. That contestant doesn't have a hope in hell anyway.

Chapter 6

"I thought you said you cleaned all day."

"Randy —"

"Okay, okay. Forget it." To tell the truth, I'm actually quite impressed by what Norma's done. The ceilings and walls are free of dust and cobwebs, and all the floors have been swept. And the floors upstairs — they're covered with something Dad called oilcloth — have been washed. She's even taken all the light fixtures down and has them soaking in the kitchen sink. She must have worked like a demon to get all this done today. Of course, I'd be the last person to tell her so.

Jim Gesner, the carpenter Dad hired to work on the outside, is up on the roof fixing the chimney. He's already replaced the broken glass, and Norma has every window in the house open, letting the fresh air blow through. It's amazing how different the place looks — and smells — this afternoon. Mind you, it's still a dump, but it's an improved dump.

"What I need you to do is go down to the basement and begin clearin' out everything you find. Lotsa stuff down there is moldy, and it'll just start smellin' the place up again when we close the windows. I've picked over what's down there and brought up what I think we can use, but most of it was junk to begin with."

Great. Junk detail. My specialty. "How do I get down there?"

"There's a trap door in the back porch that lifts up, but the steps are pretty rickety. It's better to go down from outside. There's a door 'round back."

"Where do you want the stuff I bring up?"

"Mr. Gesner said to throw it on the back of his truck and he'll drop it off at the dump on his way home."

Oh. So this place *isn't* a dump. Interesting. I turn to go.

"And Randy?"

"Hmm?"

"Watch your step down there."

I have to bite back my *What do you care?* — I'm already dangerously close to crossing the line Dad drew the other night. "Right," I say, as though I'd intended to carom around down there blindfolded, incurring as much personal injury as possible. I head for the basement.

* * * * * *

Basement is a definite misnomer here. Even *cellar* would be a tad too ethereal for the place I find myself in. Dungeon, crypt, cavern — now *those* are words that could adequately capture its ambience, but even they conjure an impression of something far larger than this damp hole in the ground. It's little more than a pit. The walls are made of large rocks balanced one atop the other. The light from the single narrow window near the wood furnace reveals someone's crude efforts to mortar the stones together — but the mortar has done little to keep out the elements or, for that matter, the wildlife whose droppings I've already stepped on. Of course, it's hard to tell where droppings end and floor begins — it's all pretty much muck anyway. And the whole experience is made complete by an intriguing bouquet that can best be compared to having your head stuffed inside a dead goat. The apple I ate earlier moves unsteadily in my stomach, and I swallow twice to remind it of the direction it's supposed to be going in.

Norma's quite the mistress of understatement: moldy doesn't begin to describe the condition of the stuff down here. Whatever isn't made of stone or glass or metal is rotten: parts of chairs, some wooden crates with smashed sides, a broken table, and a dozen other things I can't identify but were no doubt left here just so Randy Forsythe would have to dispose of them. Didn't anybody ever throw stuff out in those days?

Ugh. Every time I pick something up, the wood gives beneath my fingers like a wet sponge. I try not to think about the organisms crawling around inside that wood. I just hold it out in front of me as far as I can, and breathe through my mouth.

Although I start with the stuff closest to the stairs, it's difficult to carry because my feet slide around in the muck and I have to bend over to avoid hitting my head on low beams. On my third trip to Mr. Gesner's truck, my lower back is already throbbing and my shoulders feel as though someone's planted a steak knife between them. And the stone steps that lead up out of the basement are becoming slick with the mud on the bottom of my sneakers. By my fourth trip, I've begun cursing the house, my father for taking the sales job, and Nova Scotia for being here in the first place. And by the sixth trip, I've pretty much worked myself up into a lather over just about every adult I've ever met. I'm well into a venomous diatribe on parents in general when, on my seventh trek down those slick steps, my feet slip out from under me. I twist, grabbing blindly for the rock wall, but my fingers barely brush the crumbling mortar and I fall the last two steps, landing face-first in muck and mouse turds.

Both Norma and Gesner come running, probably because my shrieks make them think I'm being murdered. By the time they reach the back of the house, though, I'm up those steps and outdoors — gagging, spitting, pulling off my shirt, and trying to get the stuff off my face and out of my mouth without using my hands. I probably look like an escapee from a mental ward, but I don't care. I feel like I've taken a swim in a cesspool.

It takes me a moment to realize Norma and the carpenter are laughing. I mean *really* laughing. The kind of laughing that comes from way down deep and makes you hold your sides to keep from splitting them. Wheezing, honking, hooting laughter. I look up and see tears streaming down both their faces, Norma bent over gasping, her hands on her knees, Gesner gripping the doorhandle of his old truck to keep from falling down. I stop in mid-gag.

"It's not funny," I mutter, but this only sends them into further fits of mirth.

I stalk off.

* * * * * *

The air down by the water is cooler than up at the house, and not having a shirt on makes the whole experience a lot like sitting naked in front of a deep freeze with a fan blowing in your face. I shiver and wrap my arms tighter around my chest —I'm not about to put that shirt back on, I don't care *how* cold I get. And I'm certainly not about to go back up there and face those two comedians. Booker's dad used to have a saying about *sympathy* in the dictionary: you find it somewhere between *shit* and *syphilis*. How true. If I'd broken my neck, Norma and Gesner probably would've killed themselves laughing.

The grass I'm sitting on is damp, but it doesn't really matter since my pants are soaked anyway. Besides, I like it up here. I must be thirty feet above the water, where the field ends in a sheer drop to the rocks below. Only spruce trees seem to grow here, unlike the mixture of softwood and deciduous you find further from the shoreline. There aren't very many, and they're ugly — gnarled and scrubby, without many branches. The branches they *do* have are mostly on one side, and the trees all lean toward that side like they're trying to form triangles with the ground. Organic geometry. Just one more thing to add to a list of reasons why I'm thrilled to be here.

The tide is out, and the shoreline looks completely different than the evening we first came here. I read somewhere that the Bay of Fundy's tides are the highest in the world and, looking out over the water, I can believe it. Great slabs of dark rock stretch out toward distant waves that pounded over them a couple of nights ago. Beyond that, rounded protrusions reach up out of water that previously rolled away unbroken toward the New Brunswick coastline across the bay. For a minute, I find myself mesmerized by the scene, forgetting the anger and embarrassment that brought me here. But only for a minute. A gull screeches overhead and I turn, seeing again the house, Gesner's truck, and the life I want no part of. A wave of homesickness washes over me as I think of the home and friends I've left behind.

Then gooseflesh marches over my arms and chest as a fresh breeze moves across the water and up over the cliff where I'm sitting. I shiver, knowing I'll get chilled if I stay here much longer. Reluctantly, I get up and head back toward the House of Usher. I hope Dad's made arrangements for the phone to be hooked up so we can order our Internet connection. The prospect of chatting online soon with Fish and Booker is the only thing that makes any of this remotely bearable.

Chapter 7

"What do you *mean* the phone won't be hooked up right away?"

Dad stops in mid-chew, his slice of pizza dripping grease and tomato sauce over his fingers. Norma, of course, has put two dozen napkins on the table, but even all those are no match for this mess. It's probably the last time we order from Irene's Italian Take-Out.

"Look, Randy," Dad says. "I'm just the messenger here. The phone company has a list of work orders and we just happen to be at the bottom of it."

"You're not upset because you have your cellular."

"I'm not upset because there's nothing I can do about it. It's not like it's an emergency or anything."

"Not for *you*."

Dad grins. "Like if you don't get online the day we move in your life is over."

"My life was over the day you told your boss you'd take this job."

The grin vanishes. "That's not fair."

"More pizza, guys?"

We both turn to Norma who's holding up the box like it's a stone tablet bearing the eleventh commandment: *Thou shalt not argue over pizza*. I ignore her.

"What isn't fair is that in a week or so I'll be living in Hooterville and I won't even be able to make a phone call. Will we even have *lights* by then?"

"Of course we'll have lights. The power company said we'd be hooked up by next Wednesday at the latest. Maybe sooner."

"Thank God for small mercies."

Dad cocks one eyebrow and his nostrils start to widen. "You know, it won't hurt you to do without one modern convenience for a while. It might make you appreciate what you have."

What I *have* is a school where going to the washroom can get you mugged, a house that makes Alfred Hitchcock's Bates's Motel look like Sunnybrook Farm, and a social life that consists of a bloody nose and Norma. Oh, I've got a *lot* to be grateful for, I have. But I keep my mouth shut. Nobody listens anymore, anyway.

All three of us continue eating. As lousy as the stuff is, we're ravenous. We didn't get home until after eight o'clock, and I was surprised at how much we got done. I finished clearing out the basement — Norma had brought along clean clothes so I had no excuse to avoid going back down there — and she finished washing the floors downstairs and then cleaned all the windows. Together, we washed down the shelves in the kitchen. Then she started on the bathroom while I went outside and tried clearing away some of the overgrowth from around the foundation. Mr. Gesner had brought along a lawn mower for me to use, but what I really needed was something the size of those wheat combines you see on the prairies. The mower stalled every twenty seconds in the tall grass and it took me about three passes over the same ground to cut most of it, but I was able to clear out the area near the house so it almost resembled a yard. Getting it to resemble a *lawn* would take an act of God.

Dad met us at the house around six and we kept working until the light gave out. Gesner worked late, too. Dad helped him start stripping the old asphalt shingles from the roof. The weather's supposed to hold for the next few days, and Gesner plans to have a couple more men there tomorrow to start re-shingling.

It was my job this evening to pick up debris and load it on the back of his truck, a task that, as backbreaking as it was, I vastly preferred to being on the roof. Dad certainly didn't look thrilled about being up there, either. Even Gesner commented on the roof's pitch: "Sharp enough to split a raindrop," he said.

"The movers called," Norma offers.

Dad wipes another gob of tomato sauce off his chin, then asks, "What'd they say?"

"They can have our furniture at the house anytime we want, but I told 'em to hold off deliverin' it till I call 'em. No sense havin' to crawl all over it while we're workin'. We have lots more cleanin' to do."

"More?"

She looks at me, flashing that Successful Stepmother Shows Warmth smile of hers. "Gosh, yes, Randy. We just got through the first *layer* of dirt today. That place is a *long* way from clean."

And gosh, Norma, you're a *long* way from laying claim to a *brain*. "I *know* there's more cleaning to do. I'm just surprised you think we'll be able to get it all done before the movers come. I thought the whole point was to get our stuff delivered as soon as possible."

"Missing your computer, Randy?"

"Yes, Dad, I'm missing my computer." A year ago he'd never have asked me such a ridiculous question. Of course, a year ago he hadn't met Norma. "School started today, in case you hadn't noticed." The bitterness in my voice surprises even me and I expect him to launch into another "Now listen here, young man" lecture. But he doesn't.

"How was it?" he asks, leaning back and dropping the rest of his pizza slice into the garbage can by the counter. It makes a sound like a wet slap against the plastic.

"It isn't Eaton."

He sighs. "I know it isn't Eaton. But that doesn't mean it isn't a good school. What are your teachers like?"

"Lousy."

"*All* of them?"

I think of Mrs. Lloyd. "No, not all," I admit. Grudgingly.

"Meet anybody interesting?"

For a moment I consider telling him about Natalie. And about Jake and Steve. But I don't feel like talking to him right now, especially with Norma an elbow away. "No," I say.

"It'll happen. You'll see. It took a while for you to feel comfortable at Eaton, too. Remember?"

"That was different."

"How?"

"I *wanted* to be at Eaton."

He gives one of those *Not this again* grimaces that parents must practice in front of mirrors. "We don't always get what we want, Randy."

"Like *that's* a big surprise."

He sighs. "You aren't the only one who's had to

make adjustments, you know."

"I wouldn't call leaving my home and my friends an adjustment."

He leans forward, putting his hands palm-down on the table. "You're right. It's more than that. But people move all the time. They start over all the time. The thing we have going for us is that we're all doing this together."

Great. I get to hear the *united we stand* sermon. All for one and one for all. The Three Musketeers in the Garden View Motel. Give me a frigging break.

"Everything is new for Norma and me, too, Randy. Leaving life in the city. Renovating a house. Even my job. I've never had to sell anything before in my life. I don't know if I'll be any good at it."

I hate stating the obvious. "You've worked with Healthaid for years, Dad."

"In an office, sure, but this isn't the same. I've handled paper, not people."

"Why take the job, then?"

He leans back again and takes a deep breath. Like a diver about to plunge. "You know why."

"We didn't need the money *that* badly —"

He cuts me off. "I made good money in Scarborough, Randy." He pauses, glancing at Norma. She nods at him, and I wonder what it is that's passed between them. Resentment rises inside me like dark smoke, thick and hot.

Dad continues, "But I *spent* a lot, too. Eaton cost me an arm and a leg the last two years. You know that. But it wasn't just Eaton. I've been spending money all along. Too much. I thought my corporate image needed a new car every year to go along with the house in Raven Park. I never really owned a vehicle, just kept adding more to the car loan till it got out of hand. And I ended up *losing* money on the house. I paid top dollar for it ten years ago and I had to sell it well below the assessed value to get out from under the mortgage. The only money I saved is what I've been putting away for your university education, and I'm certainly not about to touch that."

My face must reveal my disbelief. "Look, I have nobody to blame but myself," he continues. "The last ten years I made some lousy decisions, and I'm paying for them."

"You're not the only one," I say.

"No, I'm not," he says softly, and I know I've hurt him. When he's really bothered by something, he gets quiet. Like now. "Maybe things would have been different if I hadn't had to make every decision by myself all those years."

Suddenly I'm thinking about my grandparents — Dad's father and mother — dying in a car accident when I was ... how old? Three? Four? And about my mother not being there anymore. Funny how I remember their dying but not her leaving. It *isn't* funny, though. Not funny at all. I feel my resentment turn inside me, becoming something else. Anger? "If things were that bad, why didn't you tell me?"

"I thought I had a handle on things. I might have been able to get back on track if the cutbacks hadn't come at work."

"Thanks for sharing all this with me," I say. This time the bitterness is intentional.

"Randy . . ."

"If things were so tight, why did Norma quit her job when you got married?"

"Because I asked her to."

"Couldn't we have used the money?"

"Yes, we could have." He pauses, looking at her again before continuing. "But I thought you needed someone at home more."

I can't believe he said that. "I *needed* someone?"

"I didn't like the idea of you coming home to an empty house."

"Like I haven't done it since I was eleven? Dad, grade *six* was when I stopped going to Mrs. Poirier's after school."

"I know, Randy, but the world's changing. Look at what happened to that teenager in St. Catharines. Violent crime —"

"I'm *not* a *two*-year-old!"

"Then stop *acting* like one!" Dad shouts, the sound big and sudden in our kitchenette.

"Look," Norma interjects, "why don't we just

leave this mess 'n take a walk through town? It's a beautiful night and I could use the exercise after that pizza."

Dad and I glare at each other.

"What do you say, guys?" Norma asks.

I don't even look at her. What *this* guy has to say doesn't seem to matter much anymore, anyway. I keep my mouth shut.

Dad looks at me a moment longer, then shrugs his shoulders. Turning to her, he says, "Good idea, honey."

"I don't feel like walking." *Throwing* something, maybe. But not walking.

Dad glares at me again, but he keeps his voice even. "Maybe not, but a walk will do us *all* good. Come on."

"I said I don't —"

"Randolph."

And that, of course, ends it. Just once I'd like to know when *I* get to make a decision.

Norma lifts four paper napkins from her lap and sets them on her plate, then pushes back her chair. "I'll clean this up later," she says as she stands.

Dad turns to her. "*We* can clean this up later," he says.

Translation: *Randy* can clean this up later while the two of them relax in front of the TV. I want to have seven kids when I get married — one slave for each day of the week.

By the time we get back, Irene's leftovers are one soggy mass, so after I do the dishes (Dad and Norma, of course, having parked themselves in front of "The National"), I scoop everything into a plastic bag. "Just getting rid of this stuff," I tell them as I open the screen door.

"Fine," Dad says.

I guess I get to make decisions after all. As long as they're limited to waste disposal.

Traffic on the street is light as I walk past the other units, listening to sounds drifting through the open windows. Most of the units are empty, now that the long Labour Day weekend is behind us, and most vacationers are already home or on the way there. Only five cars are still parked out front, and two of them are ours — the Lumina, and the Jetta that Healthaid leased for Dad. Two of the others are from Maine and the third is from New Brunswick.

I wonder whether the couple with the kid will have an easier time tonight. As if in response, a sharp wail pierces the evening air, followed by a woman's hushed voice, "It's okay, it's okay now. Shhh, you're all right."

I stop for a moment as something — a dream? a memory? — tugs at the back of my mind: *You'll be okay. Everything will be fine.* A chill zithers through me as I reach backwards in time, trying to coax the dream/memory into being. But it vanishes. Probably the lyrics of a song. One of those weepy ballads you come across on music video stations when you're channel-surfing. *You'll be okay.* The words everybody says but nobody believes.

I walk past the large garbage bin near the motel entrance. I suppose its location is convenient, but it makes a heck of a lousy first impression, especially as it's ten steps away from the Garden View Motel sign. Come to think of it, I wonder where the garden is I'm supposed to have a view of. The bed of red geraniums below the pink neon VACANCY sign hardly qualifies, and I feel in the mood for exploring. I've never really looked around the place. Besides, I've long since grown weary of watching Norma try to make sense of national news.

After dropping the bag of leftovers into the bin, I continue past the sign. I walk by the little house that contains the main office, and turn toward the grassy area between the motel and a long yellow bungalow beside it. It's darker back here and the grass is wet with dew, but the air is cool and fragrant and I really don't want to go back to that stuffy room yet. At the end of this grassy area is a high hedge, its uppermost branches faintly illuminated by the streetlights out front. When I reach the hedge, I find a walkway made of old patio stones cracked and heaved by frost, and I have to be careful not to trip as I follow them through the hedge and past thick clumps of trees I can't identify in the darkness. The sounds of the street behind me grow faint and soon I can't hear them at all.

I hate the dark, and I'm about to turn back when I hear water running and see a soft glow through the trees ahead. I keep walking and find myself in the midst of one of the most beautiful ornamental gardens I've ever seen. In the center of a large circle is a fountain that sends a thin column of water high overhead where it fans out and splashes back into a green pool. The fountain is lit from beneath, the glow softly flooding the walkway and the shrubs and flower beds that surround it. The path twists in and out among them. Two stone benches sit on opposite sides of the fountain, positioned to give a beautiful view. The area is almost entirely enclosed by the hedge I passed through earlier, and being here is like being in a dark green room. Standing just inside the hedge, I have a sudden sense of *déjà vu*, as though I've stood in this garden before. Or in one very much like it.

"Nice, huh?"

"*JEEZ!*" I literally leave the ground, my body contorting with surprise. When I touch down again, I nearly collapse on spaghetti knees. "Why do you *do* that?" I manage to gasp.

"I'm sorry. I thought you heard me coming. Really."

She's standing behind me, her eyes wide with concern. Even in the semi-darkness, I can see the shadow of a bruise on her forehead and, as my heartbeat returns to normal, it's my turn to be sorry.

"Forget it. Look, I'm the one who should apologize. For what happened this afternoon. Banging your head and everything." I don't mention the nosebleed. I'm hoping she won't, either.

"No problem. I'm so used to tiptoeing around so I won't bother the people staying with us that I forget to stop doing it. Dad calls me the Phantom." She sticks out her hand. "Everyone else calls me Colleen."

Funny. I've never shaken hands with a girl before. Not what I expected. She has a strong grip. "I'm Randy."

"You're in Unit 14."

I nod. "For the next week or two, anyway."

"Don't rush away on our account." She's smiling.

"No-one seems to be rushing at all. That's the problem." I tell her about the move down from Ontario and the house in Lewis Cove.

"I know. Your mother told me."

I force my teeth to unclench. "*Step*mother."

"Oh." She seems embarrassed, not sure what to say next. She moves over to one of the benches by the fountain and sits down.

Rather than wait for *DORK ALERT!* to flash above my head, I follow her and sit down, too. I see I was right: even in the dim light, the view of the garden from here is spectacular. Maybe this bench is what the motel sign is all about.

I grope for something to say. "You come here often?" What a dumb question. The world's oldest pick-up line. The only thing missing is a couple of drinks and some really bad lounge music.

She looks at me as though she's thinking the same thing. Then she grins. "Quite a bit."

"Did you do all this?" I ask, looking around. A lot of the flowers have passed their season, but I can see the ones that are left have been carefully placed and pruned.

She shakes her head. "My dad, mostly."

"It's nice."

"My parents used to be farmers. Over on the bay, actually. Not far from Lewis Cove."

"I don't blame them for wanting to move away from *that* place."

She frowns slightly. "They *didn't* want to. The government was squeezing out the smaller operations and they couldn't compete against the big guys. So they sold the farm and bought this place. Dad still likes to grow things, though. The hedge and fountain and walkway were already here when they bought the motel. He's done the rest. And there's a vegetable garden behind this."

"Do you miss the farm?"

"A little. But mostly I miss the bay."

I find it hard to believe anyone could miss

that monotonous expanse of water, but I don't say so. "You go to Brookdale High?"

She nods. "I missed today, though."

"I know. Norma told me about the kid. It was nice of you to help out like that."

"They needed it. They were really beat. I don't think I ever want to have kids if they make you look like *they* did. They hadn't slept for two nights. And it showed."

She smiles and I smile back. She's older than I am, maybe fifteen or sixteen, and definitely not what you'd call pretty. Her light brown hair is pulled tight in a ponytail, making her broad face seem even wider than it is. Her ears stick out a little and her chin comes almost to a point. And her teeth are a little crooked. But she has nice eyes. Maybe it's all the trees around us or maybe it's the pool's reflection, but they look to be a deep green. Almost the color of cat's eyes. I've never seen anything like them.

"Well, morning comes quick," she says, getting up. "Maybe I'll see you at school tomorrow."

I get up, too. "Maybe you will. What grade are you in?"

"Nine." She must notice my surprise. "I failed last year," she says. "Math. Me 'n algebra didn't get along so well."

"Oh." *Me 'n algebra.* It's almost like fingernails on a blackboard.

"See ya," she says.

I watch her until she disappears in the darkness, then make my own way back to Unit 14.

Chapter 8

"Now I'm going to pass out your textbooks."

I wait with bated breath. I can only imagine what marvels lie in store for us in a textbook Hensford would get excited about. It's a big, bland thing titled *The Maritimes: Then and Now*, and it looks to weigh as much as I do. A guy named Sean passes out copies while Hensford records the numbers written on the edge of each text. As fascinating as all this is, I tear my eyes away and open my book. Emblazoned on the inside cover is an epigram: *The roots of the present are buried deep in the past*. It seems like the beginning of this class is buried deep in the past. We're already halfway through our second lesson with this guy and we've only just finished going over his almighty course outline. If he has any part of this textbook on overheads, I'll scream. I really will.

The only thing that's kept me from screaming up to this point is watching Natalie. Last night, I lay awake over an hour thinking about her, wondering what she could possibly see in a guy like Jake, wondering if she knew about our little conversation in the washroom. I'd wanted to talk to her about it this morning before homeroom, but I didn't have the guts. How do you ask a person why she's dating a jerk? Especially when you've only known her one day. So I talked about moving. And our timetable. So suave.

I may have trouble talking to her, but I have zero problem staring at her. The morning sun through the classroom window bathes her in a pool of light, and she seems like someone in a Renaissance painting, her dark hair a sudden halo about her head. Every time I look at her, I feel my heart —

"Randy? It *is* Randy, isn't it?"

I look up. Hensford is staring at me like I have something he wants. An answer? A question? "Yes, sir?"

"Well?"

I can feel everyone's eyes on me. Natalie's, too. A red heat crawls up my neck into both my cheeks. I debate for a moment about whether to bluff this out, but I decide it's not worth it. "I don't know."

A couple of people laugh. Hensford cocks one eyebrow rakishly. "You don't *know*? I find it unusual

for a person not to know where he comes from."
Someone on the other side of the room titters
and the laughter grows. Even Natalie is smiling.

"I meant I didn't know what you were asking
me," I offer, both my ears burning now.

Hensford glares at me for a moment as the
laugher subsides. "Well, if you'd been paying more
attention to *me* than to Miss McCormick there,
you'd know I was saying that although this course
focuses on the Maritime Provinces, our textbook
looks at our region's ties with other parts of
Canada and with the United States. I understand
you're a new student here, so I was asking you
where you were from. Perhaps when you find out,
you'll be kind enough to share that information
with the rest of us."

My face could melt glass. "I'm from —"

"Michael," Hensford interrupts me, turning
toward a guy sitting beside the overhead projec-
tor, "would you switch on the overhead for me,
please?"

I look again at Natalie and see she's still smiling. I want to slide under my desk.

* * * * * *

"You're really racking up brownie points with Mr.
Hensford," Natalie says as we walk toward our
second period class.

"Mmm." My face is still burning. I even lagged

behind a bit to avoid talking about it, but she waited for me in the hallway.

She turns to me and I see her smile isn't a mocking one. "Actually, I was flattered by what he said. *Were* you paying more attention to me than to him?"

I look at her and blush. If any more blood goes to my face today, I'll have to get transfusions for my feet.

"Randy Forsythe, that's sweet." She lightly brushes my arm and suddenly all things Hensford are a universe away.

* * * * * *

"I'm really getting sick of carrying all these around," mutters Erin with the earrings. Her backpack sounds as heavy as mine as she drops it on the cafeteria floor beside our table. "I don't know why the office decided to hold off giving out more lockers." She sets her tray down across from Sherlyn, who is already into her second bag of chips, and slumps into a chair.

Jake looks across at Steve and grins. "Any ideas on that, Stevie?"

Steve grins back.

Erin looks at the two of them. "Did you guys *do* something?"

"Us?" Steve asks. "*Do* something?"

Sherlyn looks at Erin. "You didn't hear?"

"Hear what?"

"It appears that *someone*," and here Sherlyn looks at Steve, "poured glue in someone's lock so it had to be sawed off the locker."

"Whose locker?" Erin asks.

"Jerry Lawson's," Sherlyn replies.

Natalie looks at Jake. "Isn't Jerry the one who —"

Jake frowns at her and she doesn't say any more.

Steve, on the other hand, does. "Last friggin' time the jerk sits in *my* seat at the Regent."

"What's the Regent?" I ask.

"The movie theatre. Here in Brookdale. You don't get out much, do you?" Sherlyn asks.

"He's busy getting his house ready to move into," Natalie explains.

Jake looks at her, and the expression on his face makes me uncomfortable. "You have your own seat at the Regent?" I ask Steve quickly.

He turns to me and I can see he thinks I've got biscuits for brains. "It don't have my *name* on it, but yeah, it's mine. I sit in it every time I go to the show."

"Every time except last Saturday," Sherlyn teases.

"The guy wouldn't get up when I told him to," Steve says to me, and I can hear the incredulity in his voice. "I woulda plowed him right then 'n there but the manager came and told me to sit somewhere else or he'd throw me out. Lawson thought he was pretty smart. Until he went to his locker yesterday. 'N *that's* just for *starters*, kinda like those movie trailers for comin' attractions. When I get *finished* with him —"

Jake clears his throat and Steve stops. He looks at me and smiles, and for a moment I wonder if he's thinking about Lawson or about me in the washroom yesterday. He's seen the look Jake gave Natalie, too.

Kyle hasn't said anything until now. "But meanwhile the rest of us aren't getting lockers until someone tells who did it."

"Nobody's gonna tell," Steve says. "You know that. Least of all Lawson. In a week or two, the office'll break down 'n we'll all have our lockers. Just a minor inconvenience, guys."

"Minor to *you*, maybe," Erin says. "Meanwhile, I'm luggin' around a ton a' books."

Just then Counter-Kid walks by carrying a tray of food in one hand and his bookbag in the other. Steve nods his head toward him. "There goes your donkey, Jake."

"Donkey?" I ask.

Jake narrows his eyes. "You're just *fulla* questions, aren't you, Randy? You a narc or somethin'?"

Sherlyn throws her chip bag at him. "Give him a break, Jake. He don't know the system yet." She turns to me. "A donkey is somebody you get to carry your books all year."

I glance down at Jake's backpack. It looks like it contains as many books as everybody else's. Sherlyn follows my glance and then smiles. "Jake's got *his* books," she says, nodding toward Counter-Kid.

My face must reveal my confusion because Jake scowls impatiently. "Look," he says, "I don't give a shit about schoolbooks. Sometimes I lose 'em. If you don't wanna end up payin' for missin' books at the end of the year, you find a donkey."

"I still don't get it. What's a donkey?"

He sighs, shooting Steve a *Why'd you start this* look, then turns to me. "You find some geek you know takes care of his books. You know, always checks to make sure they're in his bag or his locker, makes sure they don't get banged around, stuff like that."

"Okay," I say uncertainly.

"Then you switch books with him when he's not lookin'. You have to do it the first couple days of school, though."

"Why?"

Steve jumps in. "'Cause geeks always cover their books. You can't switch a bare book for a covered one."

"But what if you lose your *donkey's* books?"

Steve's tone is almost scornful. "What if you do? No skin off *your* butt. *They're* the ones gotta go good for 'em."

I really can't believe what I'm hearing. It's like

everyone thinks this is okay. I glance at Natalie, but she's looking the other way. I want to know how many of them have donkeys, but something tells me I've asked my quota of questions.

Sherlyn, however, doesn't need questions to keep her talking. "Bobby's in 9-W with Monica 'n Jake 'n me this year, so that's why Jake chose him."

It's like some weird kind of underground honor. To be *chosen*. I almost shake my head in wonder, but then think better of it. "Who's this Bobby guy?" I ask, forgetting my quota.

"Super-geek," Steve says. "Bobby Hancock. They bumped him a couple years in school. I think he's supposed to be in grade seven. Maybe even six."

"A real brainer," Sherlyn continues. "Like *you*, Nat," she says, leaning across the table.

"I am *not* a brainer," Natalie replies quietly, her face red.

"Yes you are, Nat," Jake says as he puts a massive arm around her neck. "But we don't hold it against you, do we, guys?"

"What kinda student are *you*, Randy?" Steve asks, and I detect an undercurrent of something in his voice, like this is a test.

I'm not sure what to say. Somehow, the truth doesn't seem acceptable with this bunch. Luckily, Sherlyn answers for me. "Randy got in trouble with Hensturd today."

"What kinda trouble?" Jake asks.

"Sean told me at recess. Randy wouldn't tell Hensturd where he came from."

"Well," I begin, "that isn't —"

"My *man!*" Jake responds, reaching out and slapping my shoulder. "Jeez, I hate that guy. What a waste a' blood."

The others murmur in agreement, all except Natalie who is looking across the cafeteria at Bobby Hancock, sitting by himself.

* * * * * *

"Randy! I was *wonderin'* if I was gonna bump into you today."

I turn and see Colleen coming down the hall. Natalie and I are heading for our last period class — computer. I've been looking forward to it since first thing this morning. Every other teacher I've had today treats us like we don't know anything. If I were any more bored, I'd be comatose.

"Hi, Colleen."

She catches up to us and I begin to make introductions, but Natalie interrupts. "Colleen and I know each other, Randy."

"Oh, yeah," I laugh. "I've met so many people lately I keep assuming no-one else knows anybody, either."

Colleen laughs, too. I was right about her eyes — they're just as green as I thought they were. But her teeth seem more crooked than last night.

"What class are you in this year, Colleen?" Natalie asks as we continue down the hall together.

"9-S."

"Steve Carson's in your class," I comment.

Colleen raises her eyebrows. "You know Steve?"

"He's a friend of Natalie's."

Colleen looks at both of us for a minute. She seems about to say something but doesn't. Then, "Any more word on when the big move takes place?"

I shake my head. "I guess it'll happen when it happens."

"Remember, you're welcome to stay with us as long as you want," Colleen says elaborately.

I smile. "Gee, thanks."

She stops. "Here I am," she says, pointing at the room Natalie and I had math in this morning. "I hope Mrs. Newcombe doesn't groan when she sees me again. See you guys later." She waves and disappears inside.

Natalie and I continue on toward computer. She doesn't say anything more until we reach the door of the lab. "Has Colleen shown you her garden yet?" she asks suddenly. Then, without waiting for an answer, she enters the classroom.

I stand there for a moment wondering where that question could have come from. Then I go in, too.

Chapter 9

"Ouch!"

"You all right?" Dad asks.

Nothing major surgery won't fix, I want to tell him. But I just rub my shoulder and mutter through clenched teeth, "I'm fine." It wouldn't matter if I wasn't, anyway. Dad's been talking all week about tackling this project — his words, not mine — and, now that Saturday morning is here, it's going to get done. "Come hell or high water," he said. I don't know about the high water part, but this job has been hell from the start.

Who'd have thought there'd be so little of the verandah worth saving? Under the rotted floorboards we found the supporting frame in even worse shape, the worm-eaten posts and floor joists as soft and moist as towels in a hamper. "It'll all have to come down," Dad said when he saw it. So here we are now, taking the whole mess apart one piece at a time. Or, in my case, trying to avoid being hit by it one piece at a time.

I'd be safer, of course, if I kept my mind on what we're doing. All morning I've been thinking about what's happened at school the last few days. Other than me trying to avoid brain death from boredom, I mean. Some classes aren't so bad — besides Mrs. Lloyd's computer, Mr. Connors's science is turning out to be fairly decent, too — but others, especially Hensford's, are proof that irrelevance is alive and well in the school system.

It isn't classes I've been thinking about, though. It's the time I've spent *between* classes — with Jake Varner and his band of merry followers.

I've never met anyone like them. I've seen people like them, of course — you can't walk through a mall or down a street without encountering people who have absolutely no regard for the feelings of others. The ones who harass anyone who's different: old people, ethnic minorities, even kids who are physically or mentally challenged. Anyone who is, in their eyes, too large, too stupid, or even too ugly to escape notice. That's Jake Varner and his friends to a T.

I've sat beside them on the school steps and watched students change direction as if suddenly remembering something they've left behind. I've walked beside them down the hall as other kids give us a wide berth, examining the floor or some poster high on the wall. And not just junior high kids. Seniors, too. Not everyone, of course. Not the athletes, or the kids who look like they've stepped off the covers of teen magazines. Or the ones whose easy confidence makes them somehow invulnerable. Just those who are different some- how. Or weak. Easy prey.

"You just going to stand there all day?"

I look up to find Dad staring at me. "What?"

"I asked you to get me the enforcer."

"Sorry. Here." I hand him the sledge-hammer he bought yesterday at Home Hardware in Brookdale.

It feels weird to watch my father do stuff like this. The only time I ever saw him with tools in his hands before now was when I was in grade five and he helped me build a miniature windmill as part of a science project. He's wearing more bandaids this time, though — one on the thumb he hit with the hammer, and two on fingers he cut on his saw.

"Stand back," he warns.

I jump down and move a few steps back, then turn and watch as he takes aim and smashes off the single board still connecting the verandah roof to the side of the house. Miraculously, the roof stays put, sagging tight against the old clapboards. But Dad pulls on the rope he's tied to the far post and it starts to lean. "Give me a hand!" he snaps. I come around and grab the end of the rope and, together, we manage to pull the roof far enough out so it drops away in an avalanche of rotten boards and shingles.

"Jeez!" I say, the disgust in my voice underscoring the expression I'm sure is on my face. "Hard labor in Lewis Cove."

"You think *this* was hard? This was nothing, Randy."

"Nothing," I echo. My shoulder tells me differently.

He looks at me, sweat rivering down his face, and I can tell he's really tired. "It's a lot easier to tear something down than it is to rebuild it," he says. "The fun's just *starting*."

I look at the tangle of splintered wood in front of me. "Right," I grumble. "Fun. And for some *real* laughs we can rip down the *rest* of the house."

Dad's nostrils suddenly become a Rolls Royce hood ornament. "For God's sake, Randy, if it's so much trouble for you to help, then forget it! I'll do it myself!" He pivots, his back a sudden wall between the verandah and me, and starts pulling at the wood and shingles, tossing them into separate piles away from the house.

I watch him for a moment, stunned by his outburst. There used to be a time when he enjoyed my sense of humor, when he'd laugh at the jokes I made. But lately, every conversation we have seems to end like this one.

I thought it wasn't possible to hate this place more than I did the first time I saw it. I was wrong.

* * * * * *

Her back toward me as she kneels in a flower bed beyond the fountain, Colleen doesn't see or hear me coming through the opening in the hedge, and I can't resist surprising her by yelling "HI!"

She jumps to her feet, her face ablaze with surprise, but even in the yellowed light of early evening I see no anger in those green eyes of hers. "I guess you *owed* me that," she says, her hand at her throat.

"I think I owe you one more," I joke, "but we can call it square now."

She smiles. "Fine with me." She stoops to pick up a trowel and a pair of garden shears. "So, what've you been up to?"

Her question is purely rhetorical: you'd have to be blind not to realize the kind of work I've been doing. What used to be my second-best jeans are now ripped in three places, there's sawdust in my hair, and I'm wearing as many bandages as Dad. My only consolation is that he looks even worse than I do. He got to the shower first, which is why I'm here killing time.

We stopped only for a quick lunch, but you'd

never know it from looking at what we accomplished. Besides tearing away the existing verandah, all we managed to do was lay out a frame for the new floor. It took forever getting everything level and square, and whatever patience Dad had when we started was long gone by the time we packed it in for the day. He was right, though. It's a lot easier to tear something down than it is to rebuild it.

"Randy Forsythe, Carpenter *Extraordinaire*," I sigh. "At your service."

She smiles again. "You'll be glad when it's all finished and you can move in."

I frown. "I wouldn't go *that* far."

"You're not looking forward to living there?"

"Isn't there a saying about the devil you know being better than the devil you don't?"

She grins and sits down on one of the benches. "You think life on the bay is going to be hell, huh?"

I sit down beside her. "You know what I mean. I'm looking forward to having my stuff around me. My computer, especially. But I'm not looking forward to being a twenty-minute drive from everything. Especially when there's no taxis *or* buses."

"You'll just have to get your driver's license," she says.

"I still have over a year to wait."

"I'm tryin' out for mine next month. If I get it, I'll take you for a ride."

"I'll hold you to it." I look at the flower bed. "I thought this was your father's garden."

"It is. I just like to get my hands in the dirt sometimes."

"You're weird," I tease.

"No weirder than you pokin' at a computer keyboard. I bet you were on it all the time at home."

"Not all the time."

She looks at me, her expression deadpan.

I grin. "Okay, *most* of the time. But not *all*."

"There's nothin' I'd wanna do less than sit at a computer for hours. What d'you do on it? Play games?"

"Sure. But I like doing other things with it, too. Like surfing the Internet. It's cool connecting with people on the other side of the world. But what I really like is programming, figuring out how to make things happen." I turn sideways on the bench, facing her, excited to be talking about my favorite subject. "I wrote quite a few programs at my old school with a couple of my friends. Mostly games, but we even designed an office program that the school planned to try out this fall to organize their student files. They'd been using the Columbia system for years, but we found ways to improve it by —"

I stop, noticing the faraway expression in her eyes. "Pretty boring, huh?"

She looks at me. "Yeah. Kinda. But that isn't what I was thinkin'." She pauses, looking down at her hands, soil from the flower bed in dark crescents under her fingernails. "I was wonderin' how much a' this computer stuff Jake Varner and Steve Carson would understand."

Her question catches me off guard. "What makes you ask that?"

She's still looking at her hands, as if embarrassed by the dirt. Or something else. "You seem pretty thick with that bunch. I've seen you with them the last few days." She looks up and starts to say something else, then stops.

I suddenly feel like a kid caught doing something he shouldn't. I don't like that feeling. "What's wrong with that?"

She looks down again. "Nothin'. I'm just surprised. Jake and Steve don't seem your type."

I can feel my face getting red. "We're not going steady or anything," I say, and I'm surprised at how defensive I sound. She is, too.

"Look, it's a free country. You can choose your own friends. It's just ..." She pauses.

"Just what?"

"I'd be careful around those two."

I feel like I should ask her why, but I already know the answer. And she knows I know. Neither of us says anything for a long moment and, from the look on her face, I can tell she wishes she hadn't brought it up. Oddly, I'm touched by her warning. "So you don't like computers," I say, making my voice sound as nonchalant as I can.

She looks at me and smiles, obviously glad the awkward moment is behind us, then shakes her head. "I know I *should*. World of Tomorrow, and all that. But no, I don't."

"So what kinds of things *do* you like?"

"Art. I love to draw. And grow things," she says, gesturing with the trowel at the flowers and shrubs around us. "I'm a lot like my Dad. I really like animals, too. And anythin' connected with the ocean. I'd like to go into oceanography when I finish high school, but I know I can't."

"Why not?"

"Math. I'll be lucky if I get through Newcombe's course this second time around. I'm already in over my head."

I find it hard to understand what's hard to understand about math. It's one of the few things in this world that makes perfect sense. If only *people* were as easy to figure out. Especially parents. "I'm pretty good at math. I can give you a hand if you'd like."

She turns to face me, her eyes wide. "Really? You'd do that?"

"Maybe we can work out a deal."

"What kind of deal?"

"I help you with your math, and you can be my taxi and get me away from the bay now and then. Interested?"

She grins broadly, her teeth an uneven white

line across her tanned face. "You *bet* I'm interested. Now all I have to do is pass the driver's test. And convince Dad to let me have the car, of course. *That* should be a challenge."

The lowering sun casts lengthening shadows across the garden, and the bench we're sitting on feels cold and damp. My mouth widens in a yawn. "I'm beat," I say. "I'll be dead by tomorrow night."

"You're workin' tomorrow, too?"

"Isn't that what weekends are for?" I ask dryly as I stand up. The sudden soreness of my body surprises me and I grimace as I try to straighten. She must notice how stiff I am, but she doesn't comment on it. She gets up, too.

I yawn again, this one wide enough to make my jaw pop uncomfortably. It's my turn to be embarrassed. "Guess I won't be watching any late-night TV this evening."

"I hope you finish whatever you're building tomorrow," she says as we walk along the pathway toward the opening in the hedge.

"Not much chance of that. It's shaping up to be my life's work."

"What is it?"

"It's supposed to be a verandah."

"*Supposed* to be?"

"I'm waiting till it's finished before I commit myself to anything."

She grins. "I guess I'll get to see it when I come to give you that ride."

My mouth opens in another yawn, this one so wide I think of that comic strip "Sherman's Lagoon," where the shark sometimes swallows its face. "Excuse *me!*" I say. "I usually have more couth than this."

"You'd better forget *early*-night TV, too," she jokes as she turns down the walkway leading to her house.

"I think you're right," I say. "See you later."

She waves.

I glance at my watch. Dad should be out of the shower by now. I'm about to follow the walkway in the other direction back to Unit 14 when I glance behind me. Once again the circular hedge reminds me of something I've seen before, and an odd tightness grips my chest, a tightness that has nothing to do with aching muscles. I try to shake it off. After all, I've never been to Nova Scotia in my life, never seen this motel or the garden behind it. But for some reason I feel uneasy standing here. As though there's something I'm forgetting. Something important.

Chapter 10

I'm in a lousy mood. As much as I hate the idea of moving to Lewis Cove, I'm growing to hate the Garden View Motel's Unit 14 even more. Three people in a one-bedroom efficiency apartment might cut it for a day or two, maybe even three or four if everyone's on the best of terms. But make that more than a week and even Mother Theresa would find it hard not to throw things. Add a stepmother like Norma to the equation and we're talking sharp things. Lots of them. I silently curse Healthaid's lump-sum policy for transfer expenses that makes the Garden View all we can afford.

"You're early this morning."

I look back and see Colleen on the sidewalk behind me, her backpack slung over her shoulder. "Hi," I say, waiting for her to catch up, which she does easily. "How do you know I'm early?"

"I've seen your stepmother drop you off at school a couple times, but only just before the bell rings."

"I didn't feel like waiting for a ride today."

She can tell by my face the enormity of my understatement. "Oh," she says. And leaves it at that.

We walk in silence for a while, vehicles passing us as people head to work, to stores, to school. A bus with Brookdale Regional High School printed on the side rumbles past like a big yellow boat with a blue-gray wake of exhaust fumes swirling behind it. Everybody heading somewhere. Including us. Life in the fast lane of downtown Brookdale.

I'm beginning to regret not waiting for Norma to drive me — the strap on my backpack is already cutting into my shoulder. I hope Steve is right about the office giving us our lockers soon. I feel like I'm carrying a Volkswagen.

"How's the verandah coming?" Colleen asks.

"Should be finished by Christmas," I reply, hoping she doesn't feel like pursuing *that* topic any further. Yesterday, Dad and I got the floor on and part of the roof frame up, but not before we had the worst argument I can remember. All because of my attitude, he said. Like I'm supposed to *cherish* every frigging moment I spend in Lewis Cove. Jeez.

She seems to recognize this is a sore point, too. Neither of us says anything for a bit, our footsteps the only counterpoint to the traffic sounds. Then I remember. "How's the math?"

She shrugs her shoulders. "Why is there such a thing as two-step equations, anyway?"

I look at her downcast expression, sorry I brought up the subject. "Trouble with Newcombe's homework?"

"You could say that."

"Like some help tonight?"

She looks at me. "You prob'ly have lots of other things to do."

I nod. "And this will give me an excuse not to do any of them," I say, grinning. "Besides, I'm counting on you being my taxi driver when you get your license. A deal's a deal, right?"

She grins, too.

* * * * * *

"Was that Colleen Sampson I saw you with this morning?" Jake asks. All nine of us are sitting under the bleachers to avoid the noon sun, the sudden warmth having caught everyone by surprise. Only Jake in his perpetual tank-top is comfortable.

I nod. "Her parents own the place where we're staying."

"The Garden View," Steve says, stretching out

the last word so it sounds thirty letters long. Steve and Monica aren't tickling each other's tonsils today. It's too hot even for that.

Phil makes a barking sound, and Jake and Steve join in. So do Kyle and a couple of the others, and then they're laughing.

"What's up?" I ask.

Still giggling, Sherlyn leans over. "Had your rabies shot, Randy?"

I look at her. "What —"

"A real bowser," Phil says as Jake and Steve start barking again.

And then I understand.

I don't know what to say. I want to tell them that Colleen's a really nice person, someone who'd miss the first day of school just to give a couple of strangers a break from their kid. I want to tell them —

"Ever wonder why she spends so much time in that garden of hers?" Phil asks.

Steve jumps in before Phil can finish the joke. "She's diggin' for bones!"

Now everyone's laughing. Even Natalie.

I don't say anything.

I just smile.

* * * * * *

"Anything for Forsythe?" I ask. "General delivery?"

The woman in the Canada Post uniform turns to the shelves behind her. After a moment, she shakes her head. "Nope. Can't see anything."

"Thanks, anyway," I say as I turn to leave. I hate asking for mail like this. It's like you're this pathetic loser who doesn't have a friend in the world, and the woman behind the counter gets to share that good news with you every time you come in. *Nope. No-one's written you yet. And don't hold your breath. Doesn't look like they're going to.*

We don't have our own post office box. In a small town like this, you get put on a waiting list until somebody moves. Or dies. But Dad didn't even bother with the list since we won't be living in Brookdale that long anyway. In Lewis Cove, we'll have a mailbox at the end of our driveway. Dad bought it a few days ago. One with a little red flag that the guy who drives the mail truck puts up to let you know he's delivered something. That way, the whole community gets to share in the experience. *Nope. Flag ain't up. No-one's written him yet.*

That's why I like electronic mail. Just you and your computer. And the person who writes you. Or doesn't.

I half-hoped to have heard from Fish and Booker by now, but I shouldn't be surprised since I know how much they hate snail-mail. Besides, I haven't written to them either, except for the few words on the identical postcards I sent last week: *Wish you were here — instead of me.* And those postcards probably haven't even reached them yet.

I know one thing — I'm going to make up for lost time once I get online.

"Nothing yet?" Norma asks as I climb into the car.

I ignore her. If anything had come, I'd have it in my hands, right? The obvious eludes Norma.

She turns the car toward the motel where I'll drop off my books and change into my old clothes. Dad doesn't want me to work on the verandah without him there, which is good because I wouldn't have a clue what to do anyway. But there's still plenty of cleaning to be done inside the house, and odd jobs outside like digging a hole for the mailbox post, and clearing up the ends of lumber and shingles that have fallen in the yard during construction. The mess Gesner and his men have made doing the roof will take me forever to pile on his truck. *The fun's just starting*, Dad said. Right.

Norma pulls into the motel and I get out. "Don't be long," she says.

Okay, I'll be short. The incredible shrinking teenager. Since nobody listens to me anymore, they may as well not see me.

I'm *not* long. Maybe a couple of minutes, and then I'm in the car again. Norma backs the

Lumina around and drives across the parking lot, pausing at the street to check for traffic. I look up at the Garden View Motel sign, then across at the motel office. "Norma?"

"Yeah, Randy?"

"Can you wait here for a minute?"

"Why?"

"There's something I just remembered I have to do."

"Don't be long, okay?"

That line again. "I'll hurry."

And I do. In less than a minute I'm back, and we're driving down Commercial Street heading toward the North Mountain and the bay on the other side.

"What'd you have to do?" Norma asks.

I turn toward the window, watching the buildings slide by. *Leave me alone*, I want to say, but don't. "Leave someone a message."

"Colleen?" she asks.

Why doesn't she just shut up? Just shut the hell up. "Yes," I say. "Colleen."

Soon the buildings are replaced by harvest-brown fields, and then we're climbing the road that twists up over the mountain and down toward the water. She has the decency not to ask the next question. She wouldn't have understood anyway.

Because *I* certainly don't.

Chapter 11

"The old homestead's shaping up, don't you think?"

I look at my father and wonder if I should make a dash for the cellular he keeps in the Jetta. The man needs medical attention.

When I don't reply, he continues, "Well, it certainly has improved since the first time we saw the place, hasn't it?"

I look again at the house — I *refuse* to call it the old homestead — and am forced to admit that the place does look better. Gesner and his men have finished the roof and chimney, the broken door on the side has been fixed, the rotten clapboards have been replaced, and all the vehicles in and out of here the last few days have beaten down the grass and weeds so the wagon track almost resembles a driveway.

"A bit," I say. But the new verandah is little more than a skeleton, there's no more paint on the place than there was when we first arrived, and we're still two provinces from where I want to be. Unfortunately, the third shortcoming is the only one Dad has no intention of fixing.

A Nova Scotia Power Corporation truck is parked in the yard beside the vehicles belonging to Gesner and his men. They said they'd be here by Wednesday at the latest, and they actually made it. I thought getting electricity would be just a matter of hooking up a wire and flipping a switch, but there's a lot more to it than that. An electrician named Rorey Campbell has been here all day changing the electrical entrance — taking out the fuse box and replacing it with circuit-breakers — while the power guys replaced the pole that'd rotted off between the house and the main road. I think it's costing Dad a lot more than he planned because he's been pestering them with questions since he arrived. He told me he's glad he got home early this afternoon, but I don't think Rorey and the power guys share that feeling.

It looks like we move in on Friday — Dad called the movers earlier today and, as they put it, "Everything is a go." Why is it that movers and utility workmen always talk like NASA Mission Control? It's like they're all trying to be Tom

Hanks in *Apollo 13*. Looking at the house, though, even *I'm* tempted to say, "Houston, we have a problem."

Norma comes out of the house with a scarf around her head and white smudges on her face and hands. She's been painting the shelves in the kitchen, but all the white latex in the world won't transform them into those Euro-cupboards she left behind in Ontario. I'm tempted to tell her that, but Dad seems pretty stressed right now about the electrical stuff so I'm leaving well enough alone. I'm still counting the days till I'm online.

"Well, I think I've done everything I can in there," announces Norma like she's expecting the Medal of Valor or something. *Woman Cleans House. World On Its Knees In Awe.*

"Ready for tomorrow, pumpkin?" Dad asks.

"Ready as I'll ever be, sugar." She puts her arms around him and they hug while my stomach does a forward roll. The day I start calling someone names from food groups is the day I check myself into a rubber room.

Dad kisses her. "What do you say we treat ourselves and get a decent meal tonight?" I think he means to include me, but I may as well be standing here alone. I hate it when adults display hormonal impulses in public. It's like watching a toothless eighty-year-old trying to eat corn on the cob. What's the point?

"What d'ya have in mind?" Norma asks.

"Nothing Italian," he says, and Norma laughs. *Another* thing I hate — Norma laughing. When she really gets going, she begins to snort. It's humiliating. I have this fear that one day we're going to be somewhere incredibly formal, and I'll be listening to someone telling Norma a joke. People will be milling around in tuxedos and evening gowns, classical music will be playing softly, and everyone will be thinking about how incredibly tasteful and exquisite everything is — everyone but me. All *I'll* be able to think about is Norma listening to this joke. Because I know that as soon as she gets the punch line, she's going to chuckle, then chortle, then she's going to throw her head back and snort, just like a piglet at chow time.

"What's wrong with Irene's?" I ask quickly.

They both look at me.

"I was thinking of someplace with a little atmosphere," Dad replies. "The druggist in Brookdale told me about an inn on the bay not far from here. He takes his wife there for special occasions. And this," he makes a grand, sweeping gesture toward the house, "is a special occasion. Am I right?"

Anyone who can't wait to move into a place where the previous tenants were vermin can hardly be an authority on what's special. But as long as the restaurant isn't in Brookdale, I'm willing to risk it. I nod grudgingly.

"Sounds wonderful," Norma gushes. "I'll need to clean up, though."

"We all do. Just as soon as the men finish up here, we'll go back to the motel to shower and change. Till then, Randy, let's see what else we can get done on that verandah, okay?"

You'd think he was Lewis Cove's King of Home Improvement. Will this nightmare never end?

* * * * * *

I'm surprised. The place is really very nice. You'd never know it from the tacky sign out front: *The Ship's Anchor*, the letters formed from stylized drawings of anchors and rigging. The sign reminds me of the one in front of Captain Corky's, a burger place not far from Eaton Academy. But the resemblance ends there. The inn is a three-storey, gray-clapboard mansion converted into an elegant inn and dining room. Its location high above the bay gives a panoramic view of the water. The interior is all dark oak, pale rose upholstery, and white linen, and a bright fire crackles invitingly in a massive beach-rock fireplace that reaches from floor to ceiling. There are only a dozen or so tables in the dining room, but people are sitting at all but two of them.

"I'm glad I made reservations," Dad says quietly as a young man leads us to our table. "Popular place."

Norma nods. She's obviously as surprised as I am that the place is so busy. I'm glad we changed. Not that we're elegantly turned out — my and Dad's suits and Norma's dresses are still packed away on some transfer truck — but we're wearing the best clothes we had at the motel. And considering what the last few days have been like, we don't look too bad. This was an okay idea after all.

That is, until I notice who's sitting at one of the tables near the window: Jake's donkey, Bobby Hancock. He's with four other people, who, I assume, are his parents and a younger sister and brother. The five of them look even more out of place than I feel, their worn clothes almost shabby against the elegant furnishings. Bobby's father, a short, stocky, ruddy-faced guy, looks like a mafia hit man in a black polyester blazer that's at least two sizes too big for him.

But *I'm* the one who feels like a thug. I know Bobby's seen me with Steve and Jake at school, and I was with them that first day in the washroom when Steve took Bobby's five bucks. He probably thinks I'm goon squad material. I don't know why that should bother me — I haven't done anything wrong. But I *have* liked the attention I get when I'm with those guys. I know they're jerks. I wouldn't do the things they do, like intimidating, stealing, vandalizing. I'm not like them. But people in the cafeteria get up and move when Jake and Steve stand by their chairs, and they make room for whoever's with them. Me included. Kyle had said, "They're pretty important guys. You'll see." And I *have* seen. Back at Eaton, I was one of hundreds of kids, but we were all special: high-achievers, on the fast track to university. Here, I'm just The New Guy who sits near the back of his Brookdale High classrooms. But I'm also The New Guy Who Sits With Jake Varner And Steve Carson And Their Friends At Lunch Time. It's nothing to be ashamed of. But, all the same, I suddenly don't want Bobby Hancock to see me.

Moving through the restaurant, I avoid looking in Bobby's direction. It appears I've avoided looking where I'm going, too, because my left leg bumps the corner of a table near ours, sloshing water over the tops of glasses and making the table move with this loud scraping noise that sounds like someone just ripped a sheet of plywood off the wall. Pain stabs my thigh but, trying not to grimace, I glance around nonchalantly as though wondering what churlish oaf could be guilty of such clumsiness. And I find myself looking directly into Bobby Hancock's eyes.

He turns quickly away, his face red as he pokes at his salad with a fork. The rest of his family are talking and don't seem to notice how he looks down at the table, how his shoulders seem to pull in, making him look even smaller than he is. But *I* notice. And a strange feeling comes over me as I sit down with Norma and Dad at our table. A feeling I don't recognize at first because I've never experienced it before. A feeling of being in control.

A feeling of power.

* * * * * *

By the time we get back to the motel, it's after ten o'clock. Dad has to be in Yarmouth by nine tomorrow morning, which means he has to be up by five-thirty so he'll have time to shower and eat breakfast before he leaves. He and Norma, therefore, go straight to bed. I'm still wide awake, though, my thoughts on Bobby Hancock and what happened at The Ship's Anchor, so I don't bother to pull my bed out of the sofa yet. Instead, I put my jean jacket on and head outside for a walk.

As warm as the weather has been, Valley nights cool off quickly, and I pull my collar up around my neck as I walk along the row of motel units toward the street. Surprisingly, nine of them now have vehicles parked out front, all bearing out-of-province license plates. It's as though people everywhere are in on the secret that fall is the best time to visit Nova Scotia. And it is. Hot, dry days followed by cool evenings. What every tourist imagines the perfect vacation to be.

I think about Bobby Hancock and wonder if maybe I imagined what happened at the inn. The fact that he looked away when he saw me, like he was afraid. No-one's ever been frightened of me before. I —

"You're too early," Colleen says.

I whirl around to see a shape silhouetted in a window of the Sampsons' tiny house. "What?" I ask.

"School doesn't start for another ten hours at least," she says. "Get some sleep."

I smile awkwardly. I haven't seen Colleen since Monday, when we walked to school together. Well, actually, I *have* seen her, but only from a distance — across the cafeteria, at the end of a hall, passing by the window of Unit 14. I didn't try to catch up with her, not once. And I've gotten Norma to drive me to school every day since then.

"I thought I'd get a head start," I try to joke, but my words sound flat in the darkness.

"I got your message the other day," she says. Her face is a dark blob, the light from a lamp behind her casting her features into shadow.

"I'm really sorry about that —" I begin.

"Don't worry about it," she says. "I said you prob'ly had a lotta other things t'do."

I nod. I don't know what else to do.

"You still workin' on that verandah?"

"Dad hopes to get it finished by the time we move in, but I don't think it's going to happen."

"When d'you move in?"

"Friday, I think."

"Christmas is comin' *early* this year," she says.

I don't know what she means at first. Then I get the joke. "Right," I say, trying to laugh. But it comes out sounding like something else. Hollow. Like voices in a room with no furniture.

A moment passes. I feel like I should say something else, but all that comes to mind is *How's the math going?* And I already know the answer to that. I wish I could see her eyes so I could tell what she's thinking. Whether she's angry at me. If she feels ... What? Betrayed?

"Well, I'll see you around, Randy," she says and she reaches up to slide the window shut.

"Colleen?"

She stops. "Yeah?"

I stand there in the darkness like I'm waiting for a train. But I hear they don't run in the Valley anymore. And I don't have anything more to say. "I'll see you around."

She closes the window.

Chapter 12

For a moment, I think the transfer truck isn't going to make the turn. The driver is a huge bear of a man who, a moment earlier, walked the length of our wagon track shaking his head. Now, he's backed the rear end of the long, white trailer into the mouth of the driveway so it's pointing at the field beyond our house. The trailer and cab make an acute angle that reminds me of the flying formation of Canada geese. Without their mobility. I don't see how the driver can possibly avoid the soft, spongy soil to the left of the driveway where one of Gesner's men got stuck earlier this week. Miraculously, though, he does, the trailer swinging back as the cab comes around, the truck's big motor roaring against the weight of the trailer and the slope leading up to our house. Soon, both the cab and the trailer make a long, white line that eases gently to a stop, taillights parallel to our back door.

"Finally." I'm surprised I've said it out loud and I turn to see Dad and Norma looking at me.

"My, aren't *we* the impatient one," Dad comments. "I guess it's a good thing I let you miss school today. You'd never have been able to *wait* until this afternoon to be here."

"He's just excited," Norma says. "We all are." Norma doesn't miss a trick. *Seize opportunities to make alliances with your stepchild.* Chapter 8.

Dad grins in agreement. "Remember, though, the best thing we can do is keep out of the movers' way. They just need to know where the furniture and the boxes go. They'll get the job done a lot faster if we don't slow them down."

As if to underscore that point, three men in coveralls jump down from the cab as though ready for an Olympic event — *carton toss*, followed by the ever-popular *appliance drop* and *furniture gouge*. I cross my fingers hoping my computer is safe inside its styrofoam packing.

They work fast and, I'm forced to admit, carefully. Surprisingly, it's the little stuff that takes the longest, but by lunchtime they've finished unloading everything and are rolling out the driveway. Dad and Norma and I look at the mountains of boxes around us. *Our* work is just beginning.

My room is on the back of the house, a small

space tucked under the sloping roof. It's less than half the size of what I had back home. It doesn't even have a closet, so Dad bought a metal bar that clips over the top of the door for me to hang my suit and shirts on. There's so little room that my desk has to do double duty as a nightstand. Because of the sloping ceilings, I can only stand up straight in the center of the room. But as cramped as it is, it has one of the best features in the house: a window facing the bay that reaches almost from floor to ceiling. Although I don't care about all that water, I do like the way the room fills with light in the afternoon and early evening. It's less gloomy than the other two bedrooms.

The movers have put my desk in front of the window where I told them to, and I turn to the boxes on the floor beside it. Over the IBM logos are the words I scrawled in black marker two weeks earlier: BREAKABLE! HANDLE WITH CARE! And, judging from the condition of the boxes, it appears they did.

I cut through the tape sealing each of the cartons and pull out the components one by one: twenty-inch SVGA monitor (.25 resolution, non-interlaced), mid-size tower (266 megahertz state-of-the-art processor, 128 megabyte RAM, 7.0 gigabyte SCSI hard drive, 18-speed CD-ROM, an ISDN Internet connection), laser printer, and at least as much software as Brookdale High's computer lab.

I had a hard time convincing Dad to pay for the system this spring — he seemed to think my old 486 and dot-matrix printer were perfectly fine, and I spent weeks pulling up information on the Net to make him see that this upgraded equipment would be an investment in my future. I was lucky to get it when I did — the week after I brought it home, Dad got the news about his job.

After making all the connections, I turn the computer on and watch as it cycles through a systems check. I even print out a test document on the laser to make sure it's working okay, too. Then, just for the heck of it, I click on the automatic dialing program but, of course, it sends back a *No dial tone* error message. Even if there *had* been a dial tone, I'm not registered with a local server yet, but it feels good to be able to activate the modem icon anyway.

"Everything okay?"

I turn and see Norma standing in the doorway with a lamp in her hands. "Seems to be." I don't bother saying anything specific — the closest Norma gets to computers is a bank machine, and then only to make withdrawals. She's afraid to make deposits for fear they'll eat her money. Really.

She glances around my room and then at the lamp. "There's no place for this in our room and I thought you could use it. But I see there's no place in here, either."

I get up and take it from her. "I can put it on the floor in the corner." I like a room bright. I have ever since I was little. I slept with a light on for a long time. Dad said I used to have nightmares. I don't remember them, though. And he never really talked about them.

"If you've got a moment, I can use your help downstairs," Norma says.

"I've finished here," I say, turning off the computer. "I can unpack the rest of my stuff later." I follow her downstairs.

* * * * * *

"What do we do with all these boxes?" I ask. Although their contents haven't all been put away, most of the cartons themselves are empty. The living room (I prefer that word to *parlor*), hallway, kitchen, and dining room look like cardboard forests. You can hardly see our furniture, although that may be an aesthetic advantage. Our leather sofa and love seat and chrome-and-glass coffee tables look out of place in front of the faded and peeling wallpaper, as do our mahogany dining table, chairs, and china cabinet.

The only furniture that looks even remotely as if it belongs is the white kitchen table and chair set Dad got at Ikea a couple years ago. Actually, the finish on the set matches the white shelves Norma painted earlier this week. An accident, I'm sure, but a happy one nonetheless. We're sitting at this table now, the remains of a Chinese take-out from Brookdale spread before us like the D-Day of food wars.

"The movers will come back and collect the boxes," Dad says. "No charge. All we have to do is call them when we've finished."

I grin sardonically. (At least, I'm *trying* to. Our English teacher, Mrs. Pratt, is big on adverbs, and *sardonically* was one of the ones she wrote on the board yesterday. I spent most of Hensford's class wondering exactly what a sardonic expression would look like. I think this is it.) "Good thing you have that cellular," I say. "I'd hate to have to wait till our phone is installed next week to get rid of these boxes."

He smiles, the sardonic quality of my expression obviously wasted on him. "You know, Randy, there's another phone call I'd hate to see wait till then, too."

"What's that?"

"I thought you might like to call Booker and Fish tonight."

I can't believe it. "Really? You'd let me use the cell-phone for that?"

"It isn't every day we move into a new place. Promise me you'll keep it down to fifteen minutes, though. Long-distance on the cell's a killer, and Healthaid won't pay for that call."

"You bet!"

"You know where it is. You can call from the Jetta if you want the privacy."

"Thanks, Dad." I'm out of there before he remembers who usually cleans up.

The sun hasn't set yet, but the evening air off the bay is chilly. I'm only wearing jeans and a t-shirt, so I climb into the Jetta and close the door. Reaching into the leather case beneath the driver's seat, I pull out the cellular and punch in Booker's number. It seems weird using eleven digits instead of seven.

I let the phone ring at least a dozen times before I hang up. I glance at my watch: 6:40. Booker *should* be there — they eat their dinner every night at exactly 6:30. Booker's mother is fanatical about mealtimes. She thinks if mealtimes aren't regular, your bowels won't be either, and I've heard her say "You don't screw around with your bowels" at least a hundred times.

I look at my watch again, then remember the time difference — it's only 5:40 in Ontario. I punch in Fish's number, but I'm sure no-one will be home there. Fish's family couldn't be less like Booker's when it comes to time. Fish's dad often says, "We refuse to be slaves to a clock," and he and his wife have spent their whole lives pretty much proving it. They didn't even get married until they were in their early forties, and Fish was born just before his mother went through the change of life. Small wonder no-one's ever home there before eight o'clock at night.

So it's a real surprise when Fish answers on the second ring. "Yo."

"Hey, Fish! How are you?"

"Randy? Hey, Booker! It's Randy! How're y'doin', man?"

"Is Booker there, too?"

There's a click as someone picks up an extension phone. "Forsythe! How's it goin', buddy? Lots happenin' down there in Bluenose country?"

"Hi, Booker! Yeah, I'm pretty much penciled in for every world premiere on the Bay of Fundy. Jeez, it's good to hear you guys!"

"Got your postcard, man," Booker says. "That a picture of where you live?"

I think of the identical postcards I sent them, each with a photograph of the Annapolis Valley in spring, rows of apple trees white with blossoms. "The general area," I say, ignoring the dark expanse that rolls away from me to the west.

"Pretty," Fish offers.

It sounds like such a weird thing for him to say. I change the subject. "What's happening up there?"

"Same old stuff," says Fish.

"Same old nothin'!" Booker interrupts. "*Tell* him, Fish!"

Fish seems almost embarrassed. "Etheridge had a meeting with us today."

"Etheridge? You guys aren't in trouble, are

you?" David Etheridge, Eaton's principal, is almost legendary for his zero tolerance policy. Students who step out of line get no second chances. There are always ten more waiting to take their place.

Booker jumps in. "Just the opposite, man! He asked us to take over the Invention Convention this year."

"He *what?*"

"Yeah," Fish confirms, "all because of that office program we wrote. They've been using it since the middle of summer, and Etheridge is so impressed he's planning on doing away with Columbia altogether. He said anybody who could design and write a program like that would be perfect to coordinate the Convention."

"Jeez." I don't know what else to say.

There is a moment when no-one says anything. Finally, Fish continues. "We reminded him that you helped write it, too. He said he remembered and that he'd have asked you, too, if you were still at Eaton. He wants to know your address so he can write you a thank-you letter."

Gee whiz. A thank-you letter. Be still my beating heart.

"Forsythe?" Booker asks. "You still there?"

The Invention Convention. The most prestigious event at Eaton, and there are a lot of prestigious events at a school where students score higher academically and athletically than in almost any other school in the country. Being able to participate in the convention is an honor. Being asked to coordinate it is like being made king. And only senior students are ever given that privilege. Until now. I look out across the field at that god-forsaken bay. I may as well be on the moon. "Yeah, I'm still here."

"Look, you deserve to be a part of this as much as anybody. I wish you were here with us, man."

"Me, too, Randy," says Fish. "Booker and I are going out celebrating tonight. That's why he's here now. We just stopped by to pick up some cash. I wish you were going with us."

I swallow, the lump in my throat the size of a golf ball. "Well, as much as I'd like to sit and chat with you losers, I have plans tonight, too."

"You dog," whistles Booker. "Party time?"

"You bet," I say.

"With anybody special?"

"Very."

"Well, have fun, man. Talk to you soon, okay, Forsythe?"

"Yeah, man," adds Fish, "are you connected yet so we can chat? What's your e-mail address?"

"We're not hooked up yet, guys. I'll let you know as soon as I'm online. Take it easy, okay?"

"You too, man."

And then I click off the phone.

* * * * * *

"How're the guys?" Dad asks when I come in. I'm shivering, having been sitting outside for the last fifteen minutes. For some reason, I didn't want him to know I'd only talked on the phone for three.

"Great," I reply. Somehow, I'm sure the look on my face is exactly sardonic. Without even trying.

"Anything wrong?" he asks. He's doing the dishes, the chipped enamel sink filled with soapy water.

I can hear Norma upstairs, still putting things away, so I pick up a dishtowel from a pile on the counter and start wiping. I really don't feel like telling him anything. But I do. About Etheridge and our computer program. About the Invention Convention. Even about Fish and Booker celebrating tonight.

"I'm really sorry," Dad says when I finish. "I know how much it would have meant to you to be there working on it with them."

I doubt that. But I appreciate the sympathy nonetheless. It's good to be talking to him instead of arguing or listening to ultimatums. "Thanks."

He rinses a cup under the tap and hands it to me. "So how've things been going lately in school here? You haven't said much."

I think of the last couple of math classes when Newcombe showed us yet again how to balance an equation — at Eaton, we solved polynomials in seventh grade. "Things are pretty basic, Dad."

"Basic how?"

"The teachers assume you don't know anything and then work from there."

He rinses off a dinner plate. "Well, a little review won't hurt you."

I watch the suds slide off the plate, the bubbles smashed by the column of water from the tap. "I don't think it's just going to be a little review."

Dad lays the plate in the cupboard. "Now, Randy, don't be so negative. Give it time. It's only the second week."

I don't know why, but suddenly I'm pissed. What *I* think really doesn't count. *He* hasn't been sitting in those classrooms all week long like I have, but *I'm* the one who doesn't know what I'm talking about. Now, if Norma had said something was bothering her, he'd have been all over her with *pumpkin-this* and *sugar-that* and *Let's-kiss-it-and-make-it-all-better*. "Oh, just forget it!"

He turns to me. "Why do you always shut down like that when we talk lately?"

My mouth opens. "Me? I'm not the one with all the secrets."

"Secrets?"

I tell myself I'm not going to do this. That it's not worth it because he won't understand anyway. But my mouth isn't listening. "You know what I mean. The money, for one thing. You told *Norma* all about the trouble you were in a long time ago, didn't you?"

"Of course I did. She's my wife, Randy."

"And what am *I*? Hired help? *I've* been here a lot longer than *she* has."

He puts his hand on my shoulder, but it's wet from the dishwater. I pull away, and his hand drops to his side. "You're my son, Randy," he says quietly. "I just didn't want you to know what a mess I'd made of things. Fathers are supposed to fix everything. Make everything okay."

You'll be okay. Everything will be fine.

Those words again, echoing in my head. Was he the one who said them? Not that it matters. Everything *isn't* fine. And I'm *far* from okay. And I suddenly want to make him feel as bad as I do. "Did you keep secrets from my mother? Is *that* why she left?"

His eyes widen — I've struck a nerve. "You *know* why she left. We covered this ground years ago, Randy."

"All you ever told me was the two of you never got along."

"That's right," he says. "We didn't." But he looks away, down at the sink. He gropes for the dishcloth under the soap suds, finds it and squeezes the water out, then drapes it over the tap. There's more he hasn't told me. I'm sure of it.

"Has she ever tried to contact us?" I look at him closely. "Or is that another secret you've kept from me?"

"No," he says softly. "I've told you that before. Your mother has never contacted us."

I want to ask him why, but my lips won't form the words. I've never been able to ask him this question. And Dad has never offered a reason why a mother would never try to see her son. Maybe he doesn't know. Maybe there is no reason. Maybe there couldn't be.

"Is she still alive?" I ask. I don't expect him to know the answer to this. But then I see he does. It's in his eyes.

He doesn't say anything right away. Then, "Yes. I talked to a woman at that Healthaid convention in Vancouver last year, someone I hadn't seen for a long time. Someone who knows your mother. She's still alive."

Another secret. I'm angry all over again. And not just at him. "Thanks for telling me." My words are like acid, burning my mouth and the air.

"Look," he says. "That was then. Our life isn't about then. It's about now. Once we're finally settled in and things get back to normal —"

"Yeah," I mutter, dropping the plate I've wiped onto the appropriate pile in the shelf above the cupboard. The stoneware clatters loudly, but not loudly enough. I glance around the room. "Like *this* could ever be normal."

He frowns. "It could be a lot worse."

"I'm trying to imagine that, Dad."

"Look, we're lucky your grandparents didn't sell this place before they died. At least we had a place to go to."

I want to tell him what I think of his luck, what I think he should do with it, but I bite back the words and grab the last plate, wiping it savagely.

He reaches into the sink and pulls out the plug, the water making loud slurping sounds as it sucks itself down the drain. "Randy," he begins, then falls silent. He watches the water funnel down and away. "It isn't easy for me, either."

"That's supposed to make me feel better?"

He whirls around. "Would *anything* make you feel better, Randy? Or are you too busy feeling sorry for yourself to bother thinking about anybody else? We're a family. We're in this together. For better or worse."

I shake my head. "That's your *wedding* vow, Dad. Your *second* one, by the way."

"Now listen here, young man —" he begins, but I see his jaw working as if he's forcing back words. "Look, I know you think I've lied to you —"

"And you *haven't?*"

He pauses, rubbing his forehead. "I know I haven't told you everything. And that was wrong. I'm sorry. But I've never lied to you."

"There doesn't seem to be a lot of difference from where I'm standing."

His nostrils widen and his eyes are suddenly fierce. "I said I was sorry. What more do you want from me?" he demands.

"Just once I'd like you to care about how *I* feel!" I'm almost shouting. "I'd like you to care about what's important to *me!*"

"I *do* care about what's important to —"

But I don't let him finish. "Prove it!"

"How?"

"How much memory does my computer have?"

"What do you mean?"

"The hard drive. How many gigabytes?"

He flushes. "I don't know. Two? Three? What does it matter?"

"It matters to *me!*"

Dad runs his hands through his hair. "Ask me where you got that scar on your left arm, Randy. Ask me when you had chicken pox. Ask me something that's *important*, for God's sake."

I glare at him. "What did you say a moment ago? That was *then*. Our life isn't about *then*, you said. It's about *now*. Well, Dad, tell me what's important to me *now*. Try."

He looks at me, his face a mask of indecision. "This is ridiculous."

"You *can't*, can you? You don't know anything about me anymore."

His eyes harden. "I know a hell of a lot more than you think, young man."

"Oh, yeah?" Now I *am* shouting. "Where did Fish and Booker and I used to hang out? Where did we get the idea for revamping the Columbia program?" I see the uncertainty in his eyes and it makes me even angrier. "You don't even know the name of the movie the three of us went to see the night before I left Scarborough, do you?"

"Randy —"

But I cut him off. "Let's face it, Dad, you don't know *anything!*"

The back of his hand smacks me across the mouth before I even see it coming. For a brief moment, I don't understand what's happened. All I know is one side of my face is on fire as the acrid tang of saliva in my mouth mixes suddenly with the coppery taste of blood. I wipe my hand over my lip and it comes away red.

Dad's face looks like crumpled paper. I don't care. He can go to hell. "Thanks a lot," I hiss as I turn toward the back door.

"Randy —" he calls after me, but I grab my jacket from a hook and slam outside, enjoying the sound the door makes as it rattles in its hinges. I hope I've broken something. And I hope even Gesner can't fix it.

Chapter 13

The bus hits a pothole and everybody lurches violently to the left. I'm amazed that no-one comments. I'm even more amazed that many continue sleeping, as the driver gears down and gives the engine more gas, the roar almost deafening. This is my first ride on a school bus, and I mentally calculate the number of similar rides I'll have to endure between today and next June. Now I understand why school boards bus students in the first place — it obviously has less to do with transportation than with lulling kids into a numbed state of apathy that leaves teachers free to do as they please.

Which, I guess, makes them a lot like parents. I was pretty numb all weekend. Dad tried to apologize Saturday morning for hitting me, but I didn't give him the satisfaction of a reply. My lower lip looked like one of those slugs you find under old logs, dark and swollen, and it stayed that way most of the day. Norma, of course, didn't comment on it. *Know when to maintain an objective silence.* Chapter 12.

They both had the guilts, though. Norma made beef stroganoff for dinner — my favorite — and they rented a couple of movies I know neither of them really wanted to see. Both of them were action films, one a Schwarzenegger flick with more explosions than the Gulf War, and the other the latest James Bond retread with some pretty amazing stunts. Of course, the heros remained unscathed by bullets and bombs all through the movies; even their hair stayed perfect. As completely Hollywood as it all was, I enjoyed the fiction that it's possible to kick ass and not even break a sweat.

The bus pulls into the schoolyard and rolls noisily to a stop in front of the main entrance. I stand up with the others and file toward the front. Actually, I *stagger* toward the front — this backpack I'm carrying weighs a ton, and I suddenly resent Jerry Lawson for costing us our lockers. But Steve was right. The office finally got tired of waiting for someone to squeal about Lawson's lock, and they're assigning the rest of the lockers today. Good thing the principal here has never met Etheridge. Etheridge would have organized a firing squad by now.

I get off the bus just as Colleen crosses the parking lot heading toward the north door on the far end of the school. I consider catching up to her. She came by Unit 14 early Friday morning to say goodbye, but I was in the shower and Norma took the message. I feel like a jerk. And not just about the math thing. I'm about to call her name when I see Natalie come around the corner of the building.

"Hi, Natalie," I say. "Have a good weekend?" I open the door for her.

"Thanks, Randy." She smiles and my heart lurches like the school bus. Minus the pothole. "It was okay. I babysat Friday night and all day Saturday."

"Anybody I know?"

"Mr. Martin. You remember the guidance counsellor? He's a friend of my dad's."

"Right."

"He has a nine-year-old girl and a boy almost three. The boy's a real handful. I spent all yesterday recovering. How about you?"

"Nothing." Which is a pretty accurate assessment of my activities the last two days. Dad didn't even ask me to help him with the verandah. And I didn't offer. Besides watching the movies, I played around on the computer a bit, but I didn't do much else except watch waves roll across the bay. One after the other after the other after the other. The

Fundy equivalent of Chinese water torture. Jeez.

"Got your locker yet?" asks Natalie.

"I just got here. I planned to get it before homeroom, though. Come with me?"

"Sure."

The two of us head toward the office, passing Mr. Martin as he's unlocking his door. "Hi, people," he says. "Hope Cory didn't tire you out too much this weekend, Natalie."

"Not at all, Mr. Martin. He's a sweetie." But when he enters the guidance office, she murmurs to me, "The kid's a monster. I think I need a tetanus shot."

I laugh, louder than I expect. Certainly louder than I've laughed since moving here from Ontario. Come to think of it, I can't even remember the last time I laughed. It feels good.

"What's so funny?"

We turn to see Jake coming down the hall behind us. He's wearing yet another tank-top — does the guy have a thing against sleeves? Natalie nods toward the open guidance office doorway and says, "I'll tell you later."

Jake has a strange expression on his face, a little like Dad's right after he hit me. Except there's less of a crumpled quality to it. Jake's face has creases. With hard edges.

"How was your weekend, Jake?" I ask.

He looks at me for a moment without saying anything, the muscles in his neck moving oddly.

Then he puts his arms around Natalie's waist. "Woulda been better if I'd been able to see my girl, here."

Natalie pulls away from him. "Jake," she says softly, "the office."

We're in front of the glass windows and I can see Mrs. Belcher inside terrorizing some girl. At least, it looks that way from out here. The girl is all eyes as the secretary tells her something, probably to get the hell out and not come back. Surprisingly, the secretary reaches under the counter and pulls out a metal object. It looks like a lock. Sure enough, it is. Mrs. Belcher copies something off the back of it onto a long sheet of paper and passes the lock to the girl, who then hands her some money.

"Oh, great!" I say.

Natalie and Jake turn to me. "What's the matter, Randy?" Natalie asks.

"I forgot to bring the ten dollars for the locker rental. Now I'll have to wait till tomorrow to get one."

"Don't be silly, Randy. I can loan —"

"*I* got some money you can borrow, Randy," Jake interrupts. He reaches into his back pocket, pulls out a wallet, and takes out a ten dollar bill. There look to be more bills in there, too. A *lot* more. Giving me the money, he adds, "Now don't forget where you got that."

"Thanks, Jake." I'm not *about* to forget where I

got it. I suspect I wouldn't be given the chance, anyway.

* * * * * *

". . . and a number of other industries are beginning to crop up in the Maritimes, related to the raising of exotic animals and birds," says Hensford. He puts on another overhead, his seventh already, this one a copy of an article clipped from a newspaper. Beside the article is a picture of a man, presumably a farmer, standing in front of something large. I can't make it out because the photocopy on the overhead is so lousy. A moose? A kangaroo?

"As you can see from this article," Hensford continues, "some enterprising farmers in Nova Scotia are giving the turkey industry a run for its money by raising ostriches."

"Ostriches?" comes a voice from the back. Jared Fox. A real clown-type. "You can *eat ostriches?*"

"Jared, please use your hand if you have a question or a comment. And yes, you can eat ostriches. Their meat is much darker than turkey meat, and it has a rather strong flavor. But it's highly edible, and rich in protein. Some say it's more nutritious than turkey."

"I thought ostriches just laid eggs."

"Turkeys and chickens lay eggs," says

Hensford. "So do ducks, geese, quail, and other birds. We eat those, too."

"Yeah," mutters Jared, pointing at the screen. "But can you imagine gettin' stuck with one of *them* drumsticks?"

"One of *those* drumsticks," Hensford corrects, but few people hear him because so many are laughing. Jared is something of a dim bulb, but he's always good for comic relief.

When the class has settled down again, Hensford continues. "Sheep raising is another industry that's seeing competition from unusual sources. A few farmers across the Maritimes have begun raising alpacas. They're a South American mammal with wool that is stronger and straighter than sheep's wool." He shows an overhead of an animal standing beside a native South American farmer. "Although their meat is edible, the animals are raised primarily for their wool, which can be made into very fine cloth."

I put up my hand. "Mr. Hensford?"

"Yes, Randy?"

"That's not an alpaca."

He looks at me for a moment as though I've just pulled my brain out my left nostril. "I'm afraid you're wrong, Randy. This picture came from a reputable magazine whose editors, I'm sure, know an alpaca when they see one."

I can feel the class tense around me. Natalie, too. They suspect I'm not going to drop this the way Hensford expects me to. They think it's because of that incident the second day when Hensford made me feel like an idiot. Or because we're all bored to frigging tears and can't take another minute of hearing about farmers and their exotic-pets-turned-cash-cows. But they're wrong. The real reason is simpler than that. Hensford is a teacher. He has an obligation not to make errors. And if he does, he should correct them. "Those editors made a mistake, Mr. Hensford. That's not an alpaca."

Hensford stares at me. I see a muscle twitch in his right cheek. "And what makes you so sure?"

I return his stare for a moment while the class leans forward, waiting. "Because that's a llama."

He looks at the screen and then back at me. His face is red now. "How do you know?"

"Because llamas are larger than alpacas. If you compare that animal to the farmer, it must be four feet high at the shoulder. Maybe even more. Alpacas don't grow that large. And their wool is longer than llamas' wool. That's a llama."

Hensford stares at me a moment longer. "And where did you come by this wealth of information?" he asks finally.

I suddenly think perhaps I've made a mistake. Not about the picture — about correcting Hensford. I don't like the sound of his voice. It's like water — smooth, but hiding sharp rocks just below the surface. "I just know," I say quietly.

This is hardly the time to tell him I read it in *Encyclopaedia Britannica* for a project I did in fourth grade. And that I never forget what I read.

"Well, I certainly can't thank you enough for sharing a portion of your vast knowledge with us today, Randy. I wasn't aware we had our own resident llama man."

The class laughs and this time Hensford doesn't cut it short. It's *my* turn to redden, and when I finally look up, Hensford is smiling. "We all certainly look forward," he continues, twisting the knife, "to anything else you'd care to share with us, Randy."

Yeah. Like I'll ever open my mouth in this class again.

* * * * * *

"What *is* this stuff?" Phil puts his face down next to his plate and sniffs. "Smells like someone's armpit."

"God, you're gross," Monica sighs.

But Phil's right. If you've ever stood on a crowded subway next to someone who's got his hand up on the overhead support bar, you've smelled today's Tuna Surprise. The surprise will be to see how many people can actually keep it down. Or *eat* it, for that matter. I push mine away.

"Not hungry?" Natalie asks me as Monica makes room for Steve. Steve has foregone the

Tuna Surprise in favor of the spaghetti. A wise move — they can't do much to spaghetti?

"Not really," I reply.

She knows it's not just the food. "Look, don't let that creep Hensford get you down."

"Hensturd givin' you a problem, Randy?" Steve asks.

I shrug my shoulders. I want to change the subject but, before I can, Natalie explains, "He made Randy feel like a fool this morning."

"Couldn't have had to try very hard," Kyle jokes. The others laugh.

"Thanks," I say, forcing a smile.

Steve wipes spaghetti sauce off his mouth. "Sounds like Hensturd could use the treatment. Whaddya think, guys?"

Just then Jake arrives, a loaded cafeteria tray easily carried in one hand. Jake apparently has no fear of Tuna Surprise — I think there are two helpings on his plate. "Did I hear someone mention the treatment?" he asks, sitting down beside Natalie.

"Yeah," says Steve. "Been a while since we came up with *that* idea, ain't it, Jake?"

Jake shovels Tuna Surprise into his mouth and then leans back, chewing thoughtfully. "Yeah. It's a great one, too. Shame we never tried it on anybody."

I look at both of them. "What's the treatment?"

Jake looks at Steve and the two grin broadly at

149

each other. "Just a plan for evenin' things out," Steve says.

"Evening things out?"

Jake spoons more of the Tuna Surprise into his mouth. He really seems to enjoy it. Of course, he's swallowing so fast he probably isn't even tasting it. He burps, then takes a long swallow from a milkshake carton. "Sometimes, Randy," he begins, then burps again, "people need to be brought down a peg or two."

I feel like I should say something, but I'm not sure what. "Oh."

Steve elaborates. "Somebody gives us shit, we got a way to give 'em a taste a' their own medicine."

Natalie suddenly looks uncomfortable, as though she wishes she'd kept quiet about Hensford. Monica, on the other hand, can't get the details out fast enough. "Steve came up with the idea just before school stopped in June. Adults are harder to pay back than guys our age. But the easiest place to get an adult is where they live." She lowers her voice. "So Steve thought of gettin' some cowshit 'n smearin' it over their house. Enough to leave a strong impression, if y'know what I mean."

She winks and Steve and Jake's grins become guffaws. In a moment, half the cafeteria is looking at us. I turn and see Bobby Hancock, who is sitting by himself near the far wall, look quickly away.

"Wouldn't you have to worry about getting

caught?" I ask Jake when he finally stops laughing.

"Course not," he says, almost indignant. "We'd be careful. We wouldn't just start throwin' cowshit around. You'd have to have a plan, do your homework."

"Homework?"

He speaks as though to a very young child. "Once we got a target, we'd find out what his pattern was. You know, when he's home, when he's not. Who he lives with, whether he's got a dog. Stuff like that."

"Then," adds Steve, "we'd do a barn run. We wouldn't wanna get the stuff too early. The riper the better. Phil'd be our driver. He's got a four-wheeler that's perfect for this. And since the railway tore up the train tracks, the rail line is a reg'lar highway. Lotsa farms in the area are right beside where the railroad used t'be. Kyle's uncle has a barn right next to it. Right, Kyle?"

"Yeah," Kyle replies.

I look at Phil, who hasn't said anything since his comment about the Tuna Surprise. He's grinning like a kid with twelve kinds of candy. "You guys plannin' on doin' Hensturd?" he says.

"Whaddya think?" asks Jake. It takes me a moment to realize he's talking to me.

"About what?"

"Do you wanna give Hensford the treatment or not?"

My mouth suddenly feels like an ashtray. "You're not serious?"

"Why not?"

"I wouldn't —" I almost say *I wouldn't do a ridiculous thing like that,* but the look in Steve's eyes stops me. It's almost a gleam. Like the light off polished steel. "I wouldn't want to get into more trouble with Hensford than I am right now."

Phil and Steve make clucking noises, and Monica joins them, flapping her arms.

"C'mon guys," Natalie begins, but Jake cuts her off.

"We don't plan on gettin' *caught,*" Jake says, but he puts up his hands and the others stop in mid-cluck. "It's Randy's decision, guys. Let's give him some time. He may come around."

Right. And snot's a delicacy. I don't think so, guys.

Chapter 14

"You knew this all along, *didn't* you?"

"I just found out yesterday when I called the phone company to confirm our hook-up date. They said we'd have a telephone by noon today. And then they told me about the line. You were in bed by the time I got home. That's why I waited till this morning to tell you."

"I don't believe it!"

"Randy, I'm just as disappointed as you are."

"I really *doubt* that, Dad."

"I'm sure there must be some solution to this," Norma says.

"Well, Norma, if you have one, I'd really like to hear it. But since you know absolutely nothing about computers and the Internet, I doubt anything you have to say is worth listening to."

"Randy, you apologize to her right now!"

I stare at both of them. "Or what? You won't get me the Internet connection you promised me? You'll have to come up with a better threat than that *now*, won't you, Dad?"

"Young man —"

"Leave me alone! Or do you want to *hit* me again?" I stomp up the stairs to my room and kick my chair across the floor.

From down below I hear Norma tell my father, "He's just upset. Give him a while to cool off."

"He's just upset." Norma must have fallen back on her doctorate in psychology for that little observation. Well, she's wrong. Because I'm *not* just upset. I'm so angry I want to smash something. No Internet! Which means no surfing, no e-mail, no chatting with Fish and Booker online. Nothing. All because by noon today we'll be on a party line.

I didn't even know what that *was* until Dad explained it to me. How can more than one household share a telephone line? And why would the phone company *want* them to? Ah, who the hell cares? The important thing is that it makes an Internet connection impossible. *"I'm just as disappointed as you are."* Yeah, Dad. No tying up the phone line with Net time and, of course, no extra monthly payment — you must be all broken up about it. I give my chair another kick so it slides right across the floor again. Which, in a room this size, means it doesn't go much further than I can stretch my arms.

I look at the clock on my desk — 7:45. Great, the bus will be here any minute. I reach under the bed for my backpack and grab it, anger and frustration like twins in my clenched fists. I go to the top of the stairs and, hearing Dad and Norma's stupid voices drift up from the kitchen, I want to scream at them. Instead, I reach back and slam my door as hard as I can, enjoying the way the sound echoes through the house. I half-expect Dad to come tearing up the stairs but, surprisingly, he doesn't. Norma must be in Mediator Mode. Chapter 18. If I ever see that book again, I'm going to fling it as far as I can into the bay.

* * * * * *

"Hey, Llama Man!"

Getting off the bus, I turn and see Jared Fox waving at me from across the parking lot. He's with someone, some girl who's not in our class. But she takes up the call anyway. "Yo, Llama!" she screams.

I grin and wave, all the while wanting to dropkick my backpack into their faces. I could throttle that Hensford. Him and every lousy adult I know.

* * * * * *

"Hey, Jake."

The tank-top turns and sees me coming, ten dollar bill extended.

"Here's your money, Jake. Thanks."

He pulls out that thumb-thick wallet of his and slides my bill inside. "No problem, Llama Man," he says, grinning.

My fingers tighten on the strap of my backpack, my knuckles almost white. "Funny."

He shakes his head. "No," he says slowly, almost sadly, "it ain't funny at all, Randy. As a matter a' fact, I think it's pretty pathetic. A guy thinkin' he can give people shit 'n get away with it." He lowers his voice. "You know, Randy, this is what I was talkin' about yesterday. You see people give *me* shit?"

I almost laugh. The idea alone is ludicrous. "No, Jake."

"You're right. Ain't gonna happen. And you know why?"

Any idiot knows why, but I let Jake tell me anyway.

"Cause I wouldn't *let* it happen." He leans back against his locker, looking at me for a moment without saying anything, as if deciding whether I'm worth his time. Finally, "You *like* people givin' you shit, Randy?"

I redden, thinking of Dad, Norma, Hensford, even David Etheridge at Eaton, whose crap I expect to receive in the form of a thank-you letter any day now. "No, Jake. I don't like it at all."

He puts one hand on my shoulder, gripping it, and I can feel the strength in his fingers like corded steel. "Well then, buddy, you got a decision to make. What's it gonna be? We gonna throw a little shit of our own or what?"

I see Hensford's smug face in front of me. "*We all certainly look forward to anything else you'd care to share with us.*" I wonder about that, Hensford. *Anything* else? I look at Jake and smile. "Let's throw some shit."

Chapter 15

I catch her just as she's locking the computer lab.

"Excuse me, Mrs. Lloyd?"

"Yes, Randy?"

"Would it be all right if I spent my noon hour in the lab? There's some stuff I'd like to do on the Internet."

"I usually prefer it if students sign up for noon lab time in advance," she says. "That way, I know if I'll need to be here to help out." She smiles as she unlocks the door. "But *you* certainly don't need my help, *do* you? That was an impressive assignment you passed in yesterday, Randy. Perfect, as a matter of fact." She looks at me. "And I'm guessing it took you all of ten minutes to complete it."

I don't want to tell her it took me five. I don't

say anything.

She leads me into the lab. "Bobby, you have some company."

In the far corner sits Bobby Hancock, the expression on his face at least as surprised as the one I'm wearing. His hands are frozen above the keyboard and he stares at me as if I'm an incarnation of Elvis.

"Like I've told Bobby, you can leave your machine running, but please turn your monitor off when you finish. And if you go before I get back, make sure you pull the door shut behind you. I like to keep this placed locked when I'm not here." She turns to leave.

"Thanks, Mrs. Lloyd." But the door has already closed.

I look around me on the pretense of deciding which machine to use, but I'm really trying to decide what to do. I don't feel much like staying here with the kid, but I want to e-mail Fish and Booker and I'm certainly not going to be able to do that from home. *Ah, hell,* I say to myself as I pull out a chair and sit down. The computer is already on. I log on to the Net, entering the password Mrs. Lloyd assigned me the first day of school.

Behind me, I hear Bobby tapping his keyboard. He's fast. Maybe even faster than I am.

I click on the e-mail program, then enter Fish's e-mail address. Below this, in the space for copies, I enter Booker's address. I only have a little over a half-hour, so the one letter will have to do for both.

Looking at the empty message screen, I wonder what to write. I don't feel like telling them what a dump my house is, or how boring school is, or how Dad and Norma have completely screwed up my life. And I certainly can't tell them about Jake and the others and the plans they've been making since I gave them the go-ahead about Hensford. What *can* I tell them?

"Need any help?" The voice is so low I wonder for a moment if I've imagined it.

I turn around. "Hmm?"

Bobby looks back down at his keyboard, his face beet red. "I just wondered if maybe you could use some help," he mumbles.

For a second I'm tempted to tell him to take his help and blow it out his ear. But I don't. "No, thanks. I think I can manage."

I start typing, telling the guys that I'm writing from school, that I won't be getting hooked up at home after all. I don't bother with the party line explanation. They don't have to know just how backward Lewis Cove is. Booker's dad used to have a saying about isolated communities: *They're so far back in the woods they have to come out to hunt.* I never really understood the joke before, but I do now.

There are other things I thought I wanted to tell them, but they suddenly don't seem important anymore. Life in Scarborough is so removed from me now, it's like I don't even have the right to ask about it. I stare at the screen a while longer. Finally, I write that they can e-mail me at the school if they want. *If they want.* Jeez, that sounds so pathetic. I delete all this and just type *Lots to do. Gotta run. Randy.* Then I click the *Send* button and watch as the blue bar moves across the screen, indicating the message has been sent and received.

I glance at my watch. I still have twenty minutes before my first afternoon class. English. Probably another exciting adventure with adverbs. I can hardly wait.

I could surf for a while, but I don't really feel like it. Maybe I'll enter a chat-room. I turn to the screen, and I'm surprised to see the *You have mail* message waiting for me. It can't be Fish or Booker — with the time difference, they're still in class. And there's no name in the e-mail address. I download the message.

What's one thing that confuses people?

I grin, then click on the *Reply* button and type *purple.* Then I click *Send* and watch the bar do its little dance. Maybe it *is* Fish or Booker. I don't recognize the e-mail address, but Eaton may have changed its server. Maybe they're in computer class.

In a couple of minutes, the *You have mail* message appears again. I check it out.

Ode to Purple
There once was an athlete named Myrtle,
who over the high-jump would hurtle.
"The secret of winning,"
she said without grinning,
"is living a life free of purple."

Has to be Booker. He's the only guy I know who can compose limericks that fast. Usually, though, they involve a girl from Nantucket. I click the *Reply* button and type:

Ode to E-Mail
There once was a student named Randy,
who, with computers, was handy.

I pause, thinking. Then,

He programmed his Pentium
for ghostly transmissions
and received an e-mail from Ghandi.

Ugh. The couplet is clumsy. You really have to slur *Pentium* to make it work, but I've never been as good at on-the-spot composing as Booker anyway. I click *Send* and then wait.

The PA on the wall at the front of the room suddenly buzzes and Mrs. Belcher's voice comes over the speaker. *"Is Bobby Hancock there?"*

I hear the kid say, "Yes."

"Bobby, your mother is waiting for you at the office."

"Be right there." He taps a couple of keys, then clicks off his monitor, gets up and leaves.

I watch him go, then turn back to my screen. I wait, but nothing happens. After almost ten minutes pass, I click on *Mailbox* and then *In* to see the list of messages I've received. It's then that I notice the e-mail address I'm sending to is on the same server I'm sending from.

* * * * * *

Jake's been waiting for me in the hall outside Mrs. Pratt's classroom. I skipped lunch and didn't tell anyone where I was going, and Jake would never think of setting foot in the computer lab. Not of his own free will, anyway. Natalie is standing beside him, but he gives her a kiss and nods his head toward the room. She turns to me, her expression difficult to read, and then goes inside.

"It's all set," he says.

"What's all set?"

He shoots me a look and then I remember. "When does it happen?"

He grins, drawing me aside from the flow of kids in the hallway. "Tonight."

I almost drop my backpack. "What? What about doing our homework on the guy? Didn't you say —"

He waves this away. "Hensturd is divorced. No kids. Lives by himself. And he goes swimmin' at the base on Tuesday nights."

"Swimming?"

Jake sighs. "The rec center is open to the public for a fee. He goes there two or three times a week."

I'm astonished. "How do you *know* all this?"

Jake grins. "I've had my eye on Hensturd for quite a while. He flunked me last year, y'know. I been thinkin' a' givin' him the treatment myself."

The hall is almost clear now. "I have to go, Jake. What do you want me to do?"

"Meet me in the parking lot after school."

"I have to catch my bus."

He looks at me. "Not today, you don't."

* * * * * *

All afternoon I sweat about our impending soiree. *Talking* about something like this is a hell of a lot different than actually *doing* it, and by last period I've convinced myself to fold my tent and pack my camel and tell Jake the whole thing is off. That, however, is before last class, which happens to be Maritime Studies. With Hensford.

As soon as I walk in, he greets me with "I'm planning to talk about Maritime forestry today, Randy. *Do* be sure to let me know if I get anything wrong."

Jared Fox leans over and whispers hoarsely, "Way to go, Llama Man!" which, of course, everyone hears. Most of the class laughs, and Hensford allows himself a smile, too.

You smug son of a bitch. I want to see if you smile like that later tonight.

* * * * * *

"It's like this, Norma. If we don't get this project in by tomorrow, everybody in the group will lose marks. I don't care so much about me, but some of them really need the points."

"But you haven't even mentioned the project before this, Randy. And who would assign somethin' worth so much without givin' you lotsa time to work on it?"

Jake and Steve are standing beside me, listening. I've turned up the hearing-assisted volume control on the school pay phone as loud as it will go so they can hear everything she's saying. It was weird calling Directory Assistance for my own number. Even weirder talking to Norma in Lewis Cove.

"I know it doesn't sound fair, but we've only got tonight to finish it. My friend Jake said I can stay the night with him."

As if to prove the point, Jake leans over and says loudly, "It's okay with my parents, Mrs. Forsythe. I flunked last year. I can't afford not to get this in on time."

I can hear Norma thinking on the other end. Whenever she's stumped about something, she taps her fingernails against her front teeth. The tougher the problem, the faster she taps, and she sounds like a frigging typewriter right now.

"Your father won't be home till very late, Randy. Actually, he may not even be home at all, dependin' on his meetin' with the South Shore pharmacists. But I'd rather he knew about this before I give you permission."

I knew she'd say this, and I'm prepared. One of the chapter titles in her book is *Seizing the Moment — Exploiting Opportunities to Demonstrate Trust*. "C'mon, Norma, you know you can trust me."

Bingo. "All right, but call me when you get there so I know you're okay."

"As soon as I get there, Norma. Thanks."

"What about clothes 'n stuff for tomorrow?" she asks. "I can drive into the Valley to your friend's place with them if you want me to. Just tell me where he lives."

"Thanks, Norma. But Jake says he has things he can loan me. Thanks anyway."

"Okay. Hope your project goes well."

"Thanks. I hope so, too." *Really.*

Chapter 16

"Shhhh!"

Steve, Phil, and I freeze. We peer through the darkness at Jake, who stands motionless in the back yard of Hensford's bungalow, listening. Jake and I are each carrying a bucket of fresh cow manure and Steve has two. In its present state it looks more like chocolate pudding than cowshit. The odor, however, is a sharp and constant reminder that it most definitely is not.

"See anything?" Steve whispers back.

"Thought I heard something," Jake says. His voice is low, but I can still hear the excitement in it, layered and fervid.

All four of us wait. I'm suddenly conscious I'm holding my breath, not because of the manure — although that's certainly reason enough — but because I'm straining to hear above the thudding in my chest. My right shoulder throbs from the weight of the bucket, its thin metal handle cutting into my fingers. Suddenly the whole idea of getting back at Hensford doesn't seem so appealing. I'd give anything to be anywhere but here right now. Anything.

"It's clear!" Jake hisses, and they move forward as though partners in some exotic tribal dance, the kind you see on National Geographic documentaries. I follow.

Hensford lives in the west end of Brookdale, down near the Annapolis River and, conveniently, not far from where the railway tracks used to run. Monica was right. The old rail line is a perfect throughway. On the way here, Phil told me it's mostly used by joggers and cyclists and, in the winter, people with snowmobiles, but there are plenty of tracks made by four-wheeled vehicles, too. Phil said you sometimes even see cars on it, drunks trying to avoid the cops while making a liquor-store run. I was worried about meeting cops ourselves but, as Steve pointed out, "It ain't no crime to carry cattle crap." A moot point, though, I'm afraid. You wouldn't have to be a criminologist to figure out we weren't into organic gardening.

Which reminds me of Colleen on her knees in her flower bed. What was it she said about Jake and Steve? *"I'd be careful around those two."* I look at them creeping toward the house and I suddenly wish I *had* been careful. But it's too late to think about that now.

There are neighbors on either side of Hensford's house but, thankfully, there are evergreens — blue spruce, I think — planted all around his property that provide an effective screen, even from the street. The only big gap is where the double driveway leads up to the house, and Jake's already said one of us will have to stand guard there to be sure no-one sees what we're doing.

The evergreens remind me of the hedge behind the motel, just one of a million places I'd rather be right now. And, for a moment, I am. In my head, I'm standing inside the motel garden listening to the traffic sounds on the other side of that high green wall. But then, suddenly, they're not traffic sounds. They're something else. Tapping sounds? Maybe. Maybe not. I strain to hear them more clearly and then they're gone and I'm in Hensford's yard again, trying not to get cowshit on my clothes.

From a few houses over, a dog barks and I freeze again. So do Phil and Steve.

"C'mon, you turkeys," Jake mutters, "we don't got all night. The pool closes at nine."

I don't have to look at my watch to know it's close to that now. And it's only a ten-minute drive to Brookdale from Greenwood. It took us longer to get the manure than we thought. Kyle's uncle was in the barn, and Kyle spent forever getting him out of there while we waited outside in the bushes. Kyle finally took him up to the house on the pretense of getting a wrench or something for his mountain bike, and we had to leave him there. Which explains the second bucket Steve is carrying.

All three of us hustle across the yard, being careful not to slop any of our cargo on our clothes. Jake loaned me an old pair of jeans and a sweatshirt that's several sizes too large. I have to wear my own clothes tomorrow, so these were better than nothing. Still, I wouldn't want to get this stuff on me. Jake told me not to. And I'm not about to ignore any of his instructions this evening.

I was really nervous about going to Jake's place after school. The bus ride was a lot shorter than I would have liked. Although I had my choice of any place to sit — all Jake had to do was look at a seat and its occupant would simply get up and move — I couldn't really appreciate it.

I had no idea what Jake's house would be like, but I kept imagining something similar to what I'd first seen in Lewis Cove, except with three or four junked vehicles in the yard and a half-dozen lean dogs lurking about. I wasn't prepared for the long, brick bungalow with a double garage, pool, and a white cat named Cheyenne.

Nor was I prepared for Jake's parents. I

expected his dad to be a Mr. Universe type, but he's a small, soft-spoken man, the manager of a credit union in Greenwood. Jake's mother is a tall, willowy woman, very attractive and outgoing. Probably could have been a model when she was younger, if she'd wanted. She's an X ray technician at the hospital here in Brookdale. Both she and Jake's dad are very articulate, very intelligent, with a great sense of humor. Jake's the baby in his family, his older brother a lawyer with a firm in Halifax and his sister in her last year of medical school. Very high achievers.

Later, after Mrs. Varner dropped us off at Phil's so we could work on our *project* together, Jake called himself the *Varner Vexation*. I was surprised he even knew the word. I doubt if it's a name he coined himself.

"Everybody ready?" Jake asks.

The rest of us whisper "Yeah" and move into our positions. I'd hoped I could be the person who stands watch, but that job went to Phil, who, apparently, has above-average hearing. Besides, Jake says since it's my call, I get to throw the first bucket. Right now, though, it's an honor I'd gladly pass to other hands.

We agreed beforehand that doing the front of Hensford's bungalow was too risky, but it's just as well because the house is long and we don't have that much ammunition. I'm in charge of the side closest to the driveway, the one Hensford will see first when he gets home.

The house is covered with white wooden shingles that look almost pristine in the dim glow of the streetlight beyond the blue spruce. The place is nothing special, but even in the semi-darkness you can tell everything is arranged just so: rectangular flower beds with low shrubs in the front and taller ones in the back, cement walkways that look to be painted white, a pond in the back yard with a fountain that's turned off for the year. There's even a portable garden-hose carrier that you roll around the yard to where you need it. I suspect it'll come in handy for Hensford before the night is over.

Once we're all in position, we wait for the signal from Phil. And there it is, a low whistle that sounds like a cross between a duck call and a cat in heat. I look down at the bucket. I can't believe I'm here, can't believe what it is I'm about to do. But they're all waiting for me, Steve standing out from the back corner of the house so he can signal to Jake when I've started. I raise my bucket, the smell putrid, nauseating, and I focus on my target. I plan to smear the door first and then continue on up the side toward the front of the house.

For a moment, I'm not here. Not in this particular spot, I mean. I'm a few steps back, standing outside myself like one of those people having an out-of-body experience, and I'm looking at me looking at the house. I'm thinking, *He's not really going to do this. He can't be!* And then I do it. Simple as that.

Actually, *not* that simple. The manure is even less solid than I thought, and a lot more comes out of the bucket than I expect. What doesn't land on the door hits the cement step and splatters up over my legs. *"Eeww! Jeez!"* But it's too late to stop now and I plunge on, holding my breath as I stagger down the driveway swinging the bucket as hard as I can. From the other side and the back of the house, I hear sounds similar to the ones I'm making. And then I hear something else.

"Guys! There's a car comin' with its turn signal on! I think it's Hensford!" This from Phil who is already sprinting down the driveway past me, heading for the trees at the back. The rear of Hensford's property borders fields that belong to the town and lead down to the river, and I think Phil is halfway to that river before I'm able to move, to think, to run. It isn't until Hensford's headlights slice into the front yard that my brain finally unlocks my body and sends me plunging through the row of blue spruce and into the fields beyond.

From somewhere behind me, I hear the blare of a car horn and then a man's voice, shouting, but I ignore them, concentrating on the piston-like motion of my legs as they carry me through high grass and around trees that loom suddenly in the darkness. I plow through clumps of chest-high

173

bushes, and the limb of an old pine claws at my face and my neck, but still I keep running. I stumble twice and nearly pitch headlong into the earth but I catch myself both times and run faster, my breathing a series of ragged gasps that sound like sobs in the night.

* * * * * *

"What the hell do you *mean* you ain't got the other bucket?"

I swallow. I've never seen Jake this angry. It's not a pretty sight, the veins in his neck bulging like purple night crawlers, his clenched teeth making his temples swell and contract like the top of his skull's about to fly off.

Steve nods, his face a portrait of misery. "I'm sorry, Jake. I put the first one down after I emptied it, and when Phil yelled about Hensford comin', I just ran with what I was carryin'. I panicked."

Jake just looks at him. "You panicked." He may as well add the unspoken *you good-for-nothing chickenshit* because his eyes say it loud and clear.

Steve rubs the back of his neck, something he probably wouldn't do if he realized what's all over his hands. "Look, it's just a bucket —"

"Listen to me, bonehead," breathes Jake, "that bucket belongs to my father. If he misses it, he might put two and two together. This'll be all over town by tomorrow afternoon."

"Look, guys," Phil interjects, "it's too late to worry about it now. We gotta get back. If someone checks 'n finds we're not in the garage, we're screwed." He pulls the branches off his four-wheeler, rolling it out of its hiding place beside the rail line.

Jake shoots Steve another withering look, then nods his head. "Phil's right. Let's get outta here."

The trip back is certainly more pleasant than the trip out. We've rinsed the buckets in the river and, without all that cow manure to balance on the back of Phil's machine, I can almost imagine we're just a bunch of guys out for a ride instead of Public Enemies Number One, Two, Three, and Four. Almost. Somehow, though, the whole Striking-A-Blow-For-Justice thing got lost back there in our mad flight from Hensford's headlights.

It's a good thing we wore old clothes we can wash later. Jake brought a garbage bag to Phil's, crammed with stuff he told his mother was for our project but was, in fact, old clothing and the buckets. Although Jake isn't pleased with the crap I got all over his jeans, he got quite a bit on himself, too. Luckily, Phil's entrepreneur father installed a shower in his garage for cleaning up after a day of recycling. It's a cheap free-standing unit he got at Canadian Tire but, after what we've been doing, it feels like a spa. By the time Jake's mom comes by to take us home, we look pretty much the same as when she dropped us off.

"What were you two boys up to?" she asks as soon as we climb into the Varners' car.

My heart stops. I look at Jake. But he's as cool as they come. "You mean the smell?" he asks. "Phil went crazy with his cologne," which, of course, is no lie. "Squirted all of us. Twice."

Mrs. Varner wrinkles her nose. "Someone should talk to that boy about his taste in scents. What's that called, the word having to do with smell?"

"Olfactory?" I offer.

She makes semicircles with her eyebrows. "Yes, that's it," she says as she pulls the car out onto the street. "Jake's girlfriend —" She interrupts herself. "Do you know Natalie McCormick, Randy?"

"She's in my class."

"Natalie's a smart girl. She'd know that word. The guys Jake usually brings home wouldn't, though." She glances at me, then back at the road. "You're a nice change, Randy."

I don't know what to say. Jake's just staring out his window. "Uh, thanks," I reply.

She looks over at her son. "Jake, feel free to bring Randy around anytime."

He doesn't say anything. Thankfully, neither does she. She turns the radio on and we ride the rest of the way listening to some jazz festival on the CBC.

Mrs. Varner puts me in Jake's brother's room for the night. He only uses it when he visits once a month or so, but you'd think he slept there all the time. His walls are covered with certificates and awards he got when he was in school and university, and there are even framed news clippings of a couple of trials he's worked on — one has a picture of him standing beside some government official who was accused of influence-peddling. Jake's brother won the case on appeal, something to do with evidence-tampering. Impressive stuff.

I lie looking at the ceiling. I can't sleep. And it isn't because Jake's dad down the hall is trying to break the sound barrier with his snoring. I'm thinking about what we've done. I'm thinking about Hensford, what he thought when he saw the mess, what he did afterward. I've been waiting for that feeling to come, the feeling I got when I saw Bobby Hancock at The Ship's Anchor. But it hasn't. I just keep seeing all that crap running down Hensford's door.

And I see Jake staring out his car window, the town slipping past his unseeing eyes.

Chapter 17

News travels fast. Most of the knots of people in the school hallway are talking of nothing else. Hensford this, Hensford that, the mess, the stink, the people who might have done it. One girl I pass says she heard it was drug related, that Hensford cheated some dope dealer in Dartmouth and that the next time, he wouldn't get off so easy.

I look at Jake and he looks at me and, as nervous as I feel, I have to swallow hard to keep from laughing out loud. Hensford, the Druglord. It would take less imagination to picture Jared Fox, who scored one out of ten on his last math quiz, as a Rhodes scholar.

Up ahead, the door of the east wing girls' washroom opens and Monica comes out, followed by Sherlyn and a couple other girls I've seen around but don't know. "Hey! How's the Mission Impossible team?" Monica asks when she sees us.

Jake scowls at her, but not before Sherlyn jabs her in the ribs. Not terribly discreet, that Monica. Between the two of them, she and Jared might have enough gray matter to blow a gum bubble. Fortunately, the other two girls seem more interested in the contents of Jake's tank-top than anything Monica has said.

I wonder where Natalie is, but I'm anxious to find out what Hensford did last night. So is Jake. He lives only a few miles outside town, but his bus is the second run and we've both only just arrived. Turning to Sherlyn, I ask, "What's all the buzz about?"

Monica, suitably subdued, says nothing, but Sherlyn and the girls, whose names I learn are Karen and Jenna, fill us in on what we already know, with some interesting embellishments — apparently, the perpetrators scaled Hensford's house and poured cow manure all over his roof and down his chimney. Karen says that the teacher called the police, but as of this morning they hadn't caught anybody and they weren't releasing any information. Jenna has heard, though, that the police found something belonging to one of the vandals. Someone heard it was a bucket, but no-one knows for sure.

The bell rings, interrupting Brookdale's version of "Unsolved Mysteries," and I say goodbye

and head for my homeroom. Natalie isn't there —
the first time she's missed school this year. I consider calling her when I get home, but right now
I'm focusing on getting through first period —
Maritime Studies.

I barely listen to the morning announcements,
although they're usually the most entertaining
part of the school day. They're read by student
volunteers who stumble over even the simplest
words, and today one of them announces that
Brookdale Hospital is looking for girls interested
in being Candy Strippers. Everyone around me
hoots, but all I can think about is the clock ticking
over Mrs. Legere's desk: two more minutes till
Hensford's class.

And then there are no more minutes. The bell
rings and I'm out of my seat, moving with the rest
of the bodies heading toward room 114.

Hensford looks to have had a particularly bad
night. His face is ashen and lined, probably the
result of some heavy-duty cleaning into the wee
hours. I feel sorry for him. I really do. We were
idiots to pull a stunt like that.

"I'm sure," he begins, "you've all heard what
happened at my house last night. I just want
everyone to know I saw the three boys who did it."

My heart plummets, seemingly intent on
squeezing its way out the toe of my right sneaker.
He saw us! Then, when I'm able to breathe again,
it hits me: *three* boys? Apparently, Phil is gifted

with more than just above-average hearing — he and his size fourteen feet must have cleared those blue spruce before Hensford's headlights swung into the yard. I wonder for a moment if Brookdale has a track and field team, then force my unwilling ears to listen to Hensford.

". . . and although I didn't get a look at their faces, I know from their size that they must be around fifteen years old. No older than sixteen, anyway. I just hope that anyone who might know who did this will have the good sense and common decency to tell me or the police."

He glares at us for a few seconds as if expecting someone to come clean this very moment, but we all sit there staring uncomfortably back at him. Jared Fox coughs nervously.

"Jared?"

"Yes, Mr. Hensford?"

"Do you have anything to share with us?"

There is a pause. Then, "I got my homework done, if that's what you mean."

Hensford sighs. "Good for you, Jared. I don't think I need to report that to the authorities, but it *is* a remarkable feat nonetheless."

Someone snickers, and then the teacher clicks on his overhead, gearing up for yet another scintillating sojourn into Maritime Studies.

I sit there wondering why Hensford ever chose a profession working with kids. And, more to the point, why anyone *let* him.

* * * * * *

"Back again?" asks Mrs. Lloyd. She's just leaving the lab.

"Is it a problem?"

"Not at all." She holds the door open for me, then locks it with her key. "You remember the drill from yesterday, Randy."

"Yes."

"Okay. Have fun." She closes the door behind her.

"Hi."

I turn and see Bobby Hancock at the same computer he was using before. "Hi." I don't know what else to say. I feel awkward being here, especially after what happened yesterday. Then, "I came to check my e-mail. I wrote some friends back home."

He nods, his face flushed. I don't know why until I call up the e-mail program. There are three messages waiting for me. Two are from Fish and Booker. The third has no name, but the address is the school's server.

I click on the messages from Fish and then Booker. Fish's is short, just a *Hi, how're you doing?* kind of thing. Booker's is longer, stuff about school and this girl he's met, but I just skim it. I'm more interested to see what Bobby Hancock wrote me. I click on his message.

Neat limerick. I've always had a problem with

that name, though. I never know whether to pro-
nounce 'Ghandi' with the first vowel like 'ahh' (the
thing you say when the doctor sticks a tongue
depressor in your mouth), or the way you do,
rhyming it with 'candy.' I like your way better
because the other pronunciation sounds like
you're having high tea at Buckingham Palace,
nose and pinky finger pointed straight in the air.
It's the whole tomato/tomahto, thing, right? Of
course, it's not as big a problem as the difference
between Candy Stripers and Candy Strippers, is
it? Now THERE'S a pronunciation problem I'd
worry about.

I read it again, enjoying the kid's sense of humor and his whole attitude toward language. It's the first time since moving here that I've encountered somebody with the same appreciation for words I have. And that includes Mrs. Pratt and her everlasting adverbs.

I'm tempted to turn around and tell him so, but I feel stupid. After all, he can't be more than twelve years old. Not exactly the type of person I'd want to strike up a friendship with. I can hear Steve and Jake now: "What're you doin' with the donkey?" What *am* I doing with the donkey? Reading letters from a person sitting four seats away from me isn't a pastime I'd want listed beside my yearbook photo. Especially when the person in question can't go to the washroom without losing his lunch money.

But he's really bright. I mean, someone who gets skipped a couple of years in school has to be smart, but this kid's got more going for him than brains. He's got the spark. Etheridge mentioned it once in a congratulatory speech he made to the whole school after Eaton's team won a district academic decathalon. He described the spark as the difference between a student and a lifelong learner. A lifelong learner doesn't just absorb information but gets inside things to see how they work. It's easy to see the spark in people like computer programmers and mathematicians, he said, but it's also evident in people who love the intricacies of language.

Bobby Hancock is one of these people. I don't know how I know. I just do. And it feels good to be talking with someone like that again. Even if it's through anonymous e-mail.

He must realize I know he's writing me but, on the off-chance he doesn't, I don't want to embarrass him. I click on the *Reply* button and begin typing. It takes me a few minutes, but I finally finish.

> *Ode to Words*
> *Too many people think words*
> *are definitely for the birds.*
> *But history has shown us*
> *that errors would own us*
> *if not for the work of us nerds.*

Then, below this, I type two more words: *Hi, Bobby.*

I click *Send* and then wait.

After a while I hear his voice behind me, tentative, like footsteps through thorn bushes. "Hi, Randy."

* * * * * *

"...so I've been the youngest person in my class since third grade."

We're sitting over by the windows. We logged off the machines almost twenty minutes ago, and we've been talking ever since. It's funny. He looks younger than I am, but he doesn't talk that way. And it's not the words he uses. It's the way he says things, the way he *sees* things. Like a person who's had to grow up very fast.

"I bet that's been rough," I say.

He nods, but not in a self-pitying way. "It's hardest on teachers, especially in elementary school. They try to come up with things that'll challenge you but won't set you apart from the other kids. But you're set apart anyway. Kids don't much care for people who are different. It's like they're suspicious of you, like you bite the heads off lizards or listen to alternative polka music."

I grin. Alternative polka. Cool.

"What about *this* school?" I ask.

He shakes his head. "Maybe I was wrong. Maybe it's even harder on teachers at this level. Instead of teaching thirty kids, it's a hundred and thirty. How can you expect them to meet the needs of every person they see?"

"They did at Eaton," I say.

"I don't know what Eaton's like, but I bet the classes there don't have the range of ability that you find here. Or in any other public school, for that matter."

I study his face for a minute to see if he's pulling my leg. "So you think the teachers here are doing a great job?"

He reddens. "My father always says it's easier to find fault than a solution."

Bobby's words remind me of something Dad said when we started working on the verandah: *"It's a lot easier to tear something down than it is to rebuild it."* His comment really annoyed me then. It doesn't now. I nod.

Bobby continues. "Everything can be improved. This school included. But times are tough. Classes are getting bigger, money for special programs is drying up, teachers have to do more and more with less and less. I think most of them are doing the best they can under the circumstances. Aiming for the middle and hoping for the best. *Some* aren't, of course, like Hensford. Teaching is more than making overheads."

"Why aren't you going to a private school?"

He sighs. "Same reason you're here and not at Eaton. Money. My father's a meat-cutter and my mother doesn't work." He grins. "She'd explode if she heard me say that. She works as hard as anybody. There are five people in my family. I think you saw them that night at The Ship's Anchor.

"I remember."

"It was my parents' anniversary. Gina and Brad and I saved for months so we could take them." He turns to the window. "Anyway, the money isn't there."

"Does that make you angry?"

He looks at me. "A *lot* of things could make me angry if I let them. Like eating lunch alone in the cafeteria, which is why I come here. And the donkey thing."

My eyes widen. "You know about that?"

He grins. "Monica's got a big mouth. It'd be hard *not* to know about it."

I laugh out loud.

"I switched my books back the day after Jake took mine. I always record the numbers on the ones teachers give me, anyway. My parents can't afford to pay for lost textbooks."

I suddenly remember the incident in the washroom. "Sorry about your five bucks."

He flushes. "Yeah, me too."

The bell rings, surprising both of us. He gets up and reaches for his backpack. "It was nice talking to you, Randy," he says, moving toward the door.

"Same here."

"Maybe I'll see you around sometime." But he says it like he knows it won't happen. And then he's gone.

Chapter 18

"So, Randy, how'd everything go?"

Jeez! She barely lets me get into the house before she starts with the questions. "Okay," I mumble, latching the back door behind me. Then I turn and do a double take. Our kitchen is gone. At least, the one that was here yesterday when I left for school. The old wallpaper that was gray from years of wood smoke has disappeared and the plaster walls beneath it are now covered with a fresh coat of paint, a soft, flaxen yellow like morning sunshine or fresh straw. The afternoon light streaming through the window makes the whole room seem to glow.

"Do you like it?" Norma asks. I can tell *she* does — she's almost glowing herself, her face radiant despite paint smudges on her nose and forehead.

I hate to admit it looks terrific, so I don't. "When'd you do all this?"

I see something flicker across her face — disappointment? Tough. I know she wants me to *ooh* and *aah*, but that's Dad's department.

"I just finished the second coat a few minutes ago, so be careful not to brush up against it. Your father hasn't seen it yet, either. His meetin' with the South Shore people went another day, so he stayed over in Chester last night. I wanted to surprise him." She looks down at her paint-covered hands. "And you," she adds softly.

If she wants me to feel guilty, she'll have to do better than that. I walk around the kitchen, stepping over paint-splashed newspapers, and skirting the table in the center of the floor on which Norma has stacked the chairs legs-up. I inspect the walls. "I thought there'd be cracks under the wallpaper."

"There were. I filled 'em with that." She points to a container on the counter with JOINT COMPOUND printed on the label. "Thought I'd need to put on more 'n one coat, but the first one sanded up real nice."

Real nice. Jeez, she'll be saying "howdy" and "darn tootin" before long.

"So, how'd your project go?"

I look at her. "Project?"

"The one you stayed over to work on."

Right. The project. "Fine."

She looks at me as if expecting more.

"We did everything we planned to do."

"Good."

I turn to go upstairs.

"Randy?"

"Yes?" I glance back.

She looks unsure of herself, her fingers tugging slightly at the tail of Dad's old workshirt she's wearing. It's huge on her, hanging down almost to her knees. "Um, when I talked t'your dad on the phone last night, he thought it was okay that I gave you permission to stay over. He said he was glad you're makin' friends here."

Oddly, I feel as though I'm speaking to an interpreter. Would he have said this to me himself if he'd been here? I remember our last conversation, and suddenly I'm angry at him all over again. "That's real nice, Norma," the sarcasm in my voice thick as joint compound. I turn on my heel and head up the stairs.

I throw my backpack on the bed and go over to my desk, turning the chair around and straddling it with my arms over the back. I have homework to do but nothing that will take more than a few minutes, and I find myself staring out across the water. Although the sky was mostly clear today, a mass of dark clouds now looms over New Brunswick and a thick bank of fog is funnelling up the bay. That's probably the thing I hate most about Nova Scotia, the fact that the weather can change so fast. You can never depend on it. Of course, why should the weather be any different than anything else?

The phone rings: two long tones, so I know it's for us. According to the telephone company, there are two other families on our lines with different rings — one is two short, and the other is a long followed by a short. I hear Norma answer it in the kitchen. Although I can't make out what she's saying, I'm sure it's Dad. After a minute, she calls up. "Randy?"

"Yes?"

"Your father's on the phone. He's gotta stay one more night in Chester."

I wait. What does she expect *me* to do about it?

"Y'have anythin' you wanna say to him?"

Plenty. But it would only get me grounded. As if living on the bay isn't a life sentence in itself. "No."

I can hear her pause, as if waiting for me to change my mind, then her muffled voice floats up again. The sound of it tugs at my memory and, for a moment, I let my mind drift, wondering what her muted words remind me of. I gaze out the window watching the black clouds build in the west, the fog a thick gray arm reaching up the bay. Something about her voice, the darkness ...

And then I remember.

The knowing is sure and sudden, like thunder when the lightning is right overhead.

I get up. I walk to the door — three paces — and close it, trying to shut out Norma's half of the conversation, then return to my desk. But still I hear it, the sounds of Norma's words seeping up through the floor like water through a leaking boat. Looking out the window, I snap on the computer, hoping the sounds the machine makes will mask her voice and my memory. But even above the whirring and beeping of the computer I can hear it. See it.

I'm in my room. In my closet with Jerry. Jerry's my stuffed bear, but his ears are huge and he looks more like a big mouse than a bear. Like the mouse in that cartoon, "Tom and Jerry." That's why I named him that. Grandpa gave me Jerry for Christmas. Before he and Grandma went away. To that place that made Daddy cry. I don't like it when people cry. Even on the TV. Right now, I'm pretending the sounds I hear coming up from below are on the TV. Jerry and I know better. We're not stupid. But it's easy to pretend. Easier than listening to them fight.

Daddy and Mommy fight all the time now. At breakfast about the tap dripping in the kitchen sink. At dinner about the scratch on the car by the back tire. At bedtime about Daddy working late again. All the time. About everything. But the fighting about things is not so bad as the fighting about people. About each other. And about me.

"I never should have married you!" Mommy

*shouts. I hug Jerry close. When they yell, it's hard
to pretend it's the TV. I'm not allowed to watch
shows where people yell. I don't know why. TV
can't be as scary as this.*

"Then why did you?" Daddy shouts back.

"You know d —"

*I try to block out the d-word, but it slips
between my fingers. The d-word and the s-word
and the f-word, all those words go through my fingers. It's like they're stronger than my hands that
I'm pressing against my ears. I know words can
be strong. They can even make grownups cry.*

*I hear the door slam. It's like a whole bunch of
words all at once. You can't fight with a slamming
door.*

*I hold Jerry closer. He's the only thing that
makes the dark okay.*

I look out at the sky. The sun is gone now, hid-
den by the clouds above and the fog below. The fog
looks like a living thing, massive and roiling as it
moves across the water and up over the gnarled
stubs of trees beyond my window.

*I'm sitting in a garden. It's not really a garden,
but Mommy calls it that. I pretend that it is, that
it's not just a big circle of plants in big containers.
Garden plants grow right in the ground. They
don't have something holding them in. Plants like
to dig deep with their roots, reach out around them
and see what's there. That's what Mommy says.
Mommy says she's a lot like a plant, that she*

*needs to dig deep, reach out around her. She tells
me that plants are strong, that once she saw a
dandelion grow right up through pavement. She
even saw a lily push through its pot with its roots.
It was sad seeing that happen, she says. Seeing it
finally break through with nowhere to go after-
wards.*

*I'm licking my ice cream and trying not to
notice the shoppers moving by on the other side of
those plants. I can't see them. The plants are too
high. But I can hear them, their shoes making
hard sounds against the big white tiles that stretch
all the way from one end of the mall to the other.
I'm tired of pretending this is a garden. I want to
tell Mommy that, but she's still talking about
plants. About how sad they are in those big containers.*

I look at my monitor, the screen-saver flinging
colored windows at me from nowhere. I want to be
anywhere but here right now. Here inside my
head.

*She kisses me and tells me, "You'll be okay.
Everything will be fine."*

*But I don't think it will be fine. My chin and
fingers are sticky from the ice cream, and I want
her to take me home so we can wash them, but she
says there's no time.*

*"Why?" I ask. I'm trying not to cry, but I'm
scared.*

Mommy says that Daddy will be here soon.

She's called him and he's on his way, and I'll be okay here in the garden till he comes. But she has to go before he gets here. Because if she doesn't, she won't.

"I don't want you to go!" *I start to cry, not the soft, whimpering noises I make at night but big, choking sounds that rattle my chest and make me lose my breath.*

"You'll be okay," *she says again. But Jerry isn't here with me, and those hard shoe sounds on the other side of the tall plants sound like slapping noises. I'm not going to be okay.*

But she goes anyway.

I don't stop screaming. Even after Daddy comes. Not for a long time.

The colored windows keep flying at me. I reach out and click off the monitor, but that doesn't stop the images that flicker across my mind.

It isn't until much later, when Norma knocks on my door to tell me dinner is ready, that I hear the rain. But all I can see is the dark beyond my window.

Chapter 19

Maybe it's just because it's Thursday and it's
Brookdale. Or because I'm worried people might
find out who gave Hensford the treatment. Or
maybe it's because I hardly slept at all last night,
my mind playing and replaying memories I
haven't allowed myself to think about in years.
Whatever the reason, I'm in an ugly mood. But I
surprise even myself when I snap at Natalie in the
hall before homeroom when she asks me about
Tuesday night. "Why don't you ask your
boyfriend?"

She looks hurt, her eyebrows forming a single
V on her forehead. "I already *did*. I just wanted to
know how *you* made out."

I should stop now. There's a voice inside my
head telling me I'm moving beyond Dork

Territory and entering the Jerk Zone, but I ignore it. There's no-one nearby, and questions that have plagued me since the day I met her are screaming to be asked. "What *is* it with you, Natalie? Why is someone like you so caught up in stuff like what happened at Hensford's?"

She no longer looks hurt. She's suddenly angry. Defensive. "If I remember correctly, *you're* the one who was there, not *me.*"

"I was there, all right. And as much as I thought Hensford had it coming, it was a stupid thing to do."

Natalie's eyes harden and her mouth twists almost in a sneer. "It's a little late for second thoughts, isn't it?"

I look at her for a moment as if wondering what I've been seeing in her all these weeks. Besides the hair, I mean. "It's never too late for second thoughts, Natalie."

Her voice is an ice pick, thin and sharp. "What do you mean by that?"

I could drop this now, could just say "Forget it" and walk into homeroom and hope everything will stay the same as it was. But you reach a point when nothing can ever be the same. I learned that a long time ago. And I remembered it again last night.

"What in hell can you possibly see in Jake Varner?"

Her eyes flash. "What business is it of *yours?*

Who do you think you *are*, anyway?" she asks, almost spitting the words. People down the hall from us turn and stare as Natalie spins on her heel and stalks off.

I consider just letting her go, but I've bypassed Jerk Zone and plunged headlong into Idiot City. Without passing GO or collecting two hundred dollars. What do I have to lose, anyway?

I follow her as she clatters down the stairs and out the exit, catching up to her halfway across the side yard. "Natalie!"

She ignores me, her back an iron rod as she hurries across the driveway toward the soccer field.

"Natalie!" I run in front of her. She stops, and in her face I see something more than anger. Humiliation?

"I'm sorry I upset you," I say. "But I'm not sorry for the question."

She looks away, but not before I see her eyes glistening. "You don't have the right —" she begins softly, but I cut her off.

"Look, I know I don't have the right. But I'd still like to know. We're friends, aren't we?"

She looks at me without saying anything.

I'm not sure if her silence indicates agreement or something else, but I don't wait for clarification. "You just don't put me in mind of the kind of person who'd get mixed up with Jake and Steve and their games."

"And what kind of person *is* that? Enlighten me, Randy. What kind of person would get mixed up in throwing cow manure all over a teacher's house?"

I'm grateful that she's dropped her voice to a whisper. Now it's my turn to feel defensive, but I swallow hard and try again. "Like I said, it was stupid. Worse than stupid. I should have known better. I could try to blame it on a bunch of things, but *I* was the person who did it. And I regret it. I don't think I *am* that kind of person. And I don't think *you* are, either."

She looks down at her feet. "What makes you so sure?" she asks so softly I can barely hear her.

"The way you looked at Jake just before he and Steve and the others took me to the washroom the first day of school. You *knew* what was going to happen there, didn't you?"

She doesn't say anything. She doesn't have to.

"And the way you looked at him Tuesday afternoon, when he met me in the hall to say we were going to give Hensford the treatment."

She moves over to the bleachers and sits down. I follow her.

"What is it about Jake?" I continue. "You're beautiful. You're smart. You're funny. You could have any guy you want —"

"That's where you're wrong," she interrupts. There are tears in her eyes again. "Jake's the only guy I've ever dated."

"I don't believe that."

"I don't care *what* you believe. It's the truth. Guys don't ask me out."

"Who *would*, with Jake around?"

"I'm talking about *before* Jake. No-one did. All my friends were dating by the end of grade seven, and I was sitting home watching TV. Or doing schoolwork or playing with the computer. I used to wonder what was wrong with me."

"There's *nothing* wrong with you."

She looks out over the grass toward the school. "Yes, there is. I'm smart." She turns to me again. "I don't mean that the way it sounds, like I'm bragging. It's just that it's easier for a guy to be smart." She sees me about to disagree. "Would *you* want to date a girl who always made higher marks than you? Always beat you on tests? Always did better on assignments and projects? *Would* you?"

I think about this for a moment. Before I can answer, though, she continues. "Jake is the first guy who didn't care. I guess when you've flunked as many times as he has, you stop giving a damn."

I remember something Jake's mother said: *"Natalie's a smart girl. She'd know that word."* Perhaps there's another reason Jake asked her out, but I don't say this. Instead — "You must have known what he was like from the start, Natalie."

"Of course I did. But I guess I thought I could change him, you know?" She looks down at her hands. "Sometimes I *still* think I can."

"And you're not worried that *he'll* change *you*?"

The anger is back. "I can be *with* Jake without being *like* him."

I recall the way she laughed along with the others when they made fun of Colleen and I know this isn't true. It wasn't true for me, either. Hensford's house is proof of that. Natalie McCormick isn't the person she thinks she is. Nor am I. And I'm only now realizing both of these things.

"Now isn't *this* a picture?" Both of us jump, turning toward the voice behind us. As if we've conjured him, Jake is standing there, his face a strange mix of expressions, each sliding into the next before a single one can take form.

Both of us get up. "You startled us, Jake," says Natalie.

"Yeah," he says. Nothing else.

I wonder how much he's heard. Even without looking at Natalie, I can tell she's wondering the same thing. "Where *were* you?" she asks. "I couldn't find you this morning."

"I need to talk to Randy," he says. I don't like the sound of his voice. There's something almost compendious about it, a dam holding back a river of words.

"What about?" I ask.

Just then the bell rings. The three of us stand there like we're each waiting for someone else to make the first move. It's Jake who does. "Nat, you better get to homeroom. Tell Legere that Randy'll be there in a minute."

"I can wait —" she begins, but he just waves her off with his hand. "We'll just be a minute," he says. But he isn't looking at her. He's looking at me the whole time.

She hesitates, turning to him and then me. Finally, "Don't be long, okay?" She hurries toward the school.

"So, what's up, Jake?"

He looks at me. "I was just about to ask you that same question," he says slowly.

I swallow. For the first time, Jake isn't wearing a tank-top. The sun has no heat today after that rain last night, and he's wearing a hooded sweat-shirt with the words *No pain, No gain* on it. Somehow, the loose-fitting sweatshirt is even more intimidating than his tank-tops. You don't have to see his muscles to recognize the strength in his arms and shoulders. It's the way he stands, the way he holds himself, like he's completely com-fortable inside his skin. Completely not the way *I* feel right now — like a toothpick with legs. A toothpick he could snap without trying.

I want to make a joke but I can't find the words. It seems, though, that Jake has plenty to say. "I just came from Baxter's office."

"The vice-principal?" I ask.

He nods. "The cops were there, too. So was Hensford."

My heart staggers in my chest, and I almost have to will it to start beating again. "What did they say?"

He shakes his head as if he really can't believe my stupidity. "Now, what d'you *think* they said, Randy?"

"They know?" I can barely get the words out. I'm speaking through sand, hot and dry.

"Yeah. They know." He shoves his hands in his pockets, shifting his weight to one hip. "Seems my dad put his initials on the bottom of that bucket."

The bucket Steve left behind. Jeez, I can barely breathe.

"There's fifty-three people in the *V* section of the phone book. The cops counted 'em. But they said there's only one with the first initial A."

I think of Jake's father's name. Alan. This time I can't even swallow.

"They call him?" I ask.

"Yeah. They called him. And guess what? He was missin' a bucket. I tried to tell my dad I didn't take it — I mean, anyone could've stolen it, right? — but he reminded me that only family had keys to his toolshed, and the lock wasn't broken."

In the distance, I can hear the morning announcements begin. They're muted, much like the words Jake is saying now. I can hardly hear them above the rush of blood in my ears. I try to concentrate, try to make sense of them as they flow over me, around me. Finally, I hear him say something about a game show and I grab it like a life line. "Jeopardy?"

"Double jeopardy," he repeats. "It means gettin' two punishments for the same crime. The school ain't gonna do nothin' to me because the police are involved. If they did, a judge might throw it out of court because the school already punished me."

I'm surprised at how much he knows about these things. Then I remember who's standing here telling me this. "So," I say, "when'll they be calling the rest of us to the office?"

Jake shakes his head. "They won't."

Now I'm *really* surprised. "They won't?"

"They only know about me."

He sees the question on my face. "I said I did it alone."

I suddenly think of a project I did at Eaton on investigative journalism. We had to look at any major news event in the last fifty years, and I chose the assassination of the American president, John F. Kennedy. I waded through tons of material on Lee Harvey Oswald, the man who killed him, and I had to laugh when I read the Warren Commission's finding that Oswald acted alone. I almost want to laugh now. "Hensford *saw* us. All except Phil. Hensford *knows* there were at least three of us there. The police must know, too."

Jake's face fills with contempt. "They may *know* it, but there ain't a hell of a lot they can *do* about it if I'm tellin' 'em I did it alone. And *that's* what I'm tellin' 'em."

I can almost breathe again. "Thanks, Jake."

He looks at me and smiles, but his eyes are granite. "That's what friends are for. Right, buddy?"

"Right." I think.

"Now, there's somethin' *you* can do for *me*," he says. "Friend."

* * * * * *

"You're becoming a regular, Randy," Mrs. Lloyd says.

I try to smile, but I'm sure my expression looks more like a grimace. "I remember about the door thing," I tell her.

She nods. "Have fun." And then she's gone.

I'm surprised to find myself alone. I need someone to talk to and I'd hoped Bobby would be here. There's no-one else to turn to. Certainly no-one in the group, not even Natalie after what happened this morning. I thought about Colleen, but I feel like such a fool, especially after she warned me about Jake in the first place. And after the way I treated her.

I don't know what I expected to tell Bobby. Maybe nothing. Maybe everything. For some reason, I think he's the only person who will understand. Natalie was wrong when she said it's easier for a guy to be smart. I thought about

Bobby when she said that. It may be easier for *some* guys, but not all of them. I remember the school I went to before Eaton, an ordinary public school with kids up to grade six. At the closing ceremony they held every June, the school would present awards for all kinds of things. Most Improved awards, Citizenship awards, awards for Outstanding Athlete — all kinds of things, including Highest Standing.

It was weird watching the winners go up to the stage. Kids going up for any of the non-academic awards would strut like Sylvester Stallone in that old *Rocky* film, heads high, arms raised in victory. Kids going up for Highest Standing or Most Improved or any other academic award would slouch across the stage with their heads down as though approaching a guillotine.

I was one of those kids. I remember Dad talking to me about it. He'd come to the closing at the end of my grade six, and that evening he asked me what I had to be ashamed of. At the time, I didn't understand the question and I said "Nothing." The next day when he came home from work, he told me about Eaton, about how it was different from other schools, and that I'd be going there in the fall.

I imagine him asking me that same question again. "What do you have to be ashamed of, Randy?" Then I imagine his face when I give him my answer now.

Chapter 20

The waves are gray and relentless. I wonder briefly about their color, how they can be gray when the sky above is so blue. But it suits my situation. Gray. Deepening to black.

From far off I hear someone calling. I turn and see Norma standing by the house with her hands cupped around her mouth. I can't hear everything she's saying because the wind snatches her words and flings them back to her. All I can make out is "father" and "telephone." I get up and start to run.

"Hi, Dad?" I say when I make it to the phone. My words sound louder than they need to be. I'm out of breath.

"Hi, Randy," he says. "How are things?"

"Okay," I lie. "How're things with you?"

"Okay."

I hate this little dance that grownups get you into when they begin conversations. It's like standing in an echo chamber. Nobody knows what to say so they just repeat each other, in words no longer than two syllables. It makes you feel like shouting "precipitate" and "appendectomy," just for the heck of it. But it's good to be talking to Dad again. Especially now.

"Norma says she's got a surprise for me when I get back."

I look around me at the sunny kitchen. "She's right."

"Any hints?"

"What do *you* think?" I ask. Dad could never stand surprises. He was always the kind of guy who'd needle you to death for clues about presents you'd bought him or movies you'd watched that he might like to see. He hasn't done that to me for a long time. I find myself wondering when it stopped. And why.

"Everything okay at school?"

It's like he's read my mind. *No*, I want to tell him. *Everything's not okay. And I don't know what to do about it.* But I can't tell him that. Not now. Not with all this distance between us. A distance measured by more than telephone wires.

"Sure," I say softly. "Everything's fine." But now there's a lump in my throat, and I can't swallow it away.

"How's the weather over there?" he asks.

I look down at the phone, my eyes passing over the letters on the keypad. When I was little, I used to think those three-letter combinations were words, some secret code. Dad has a secret code, too. One he probably isn't even aware of.

From the time I was nine till I turned twelve, I went to summer camp at Lake Watokwa, an hour's drive from home. Dad would call two or three times while I was there, usually to ask if there was anything I needed. At first I was annoyed, embarrassed that he was treating me like such a baby, but soon I understood the real reason for his calls. He was lonely. Near the end of every conversation, when he was groping for things to say just to stay on the line, he'd haul out that old standby: "How's the weather over there?" And then I would know how much he was missing me.

Suddenly I feel my throat close over — I'm ten years old again, holding a phone at Lake Watokwa while Dad, on the other end, asks me if it's been raining; I'm six years old, trick-or-treating at someone's front door with Dad standing in the shadows behind me; I'm four, clinging fiercely to him in a mall, desperately afraid that, if I let go, he'll leave me behind, too. I blink several times, afraid Norma will see the tears that come from nowhere.

"Dad?"

"Yes, Randy?"

I struggle to keep my voice even. I want so much to tell him everything. About what's happened. What I've done. And, more importantly, about Jake. "When will you be home?"

"I already told Norma that I have to stay in Chester one more night. My appointment turned into four. The pharmacists on the South Shore are very interested in Healthaid's group sales policy, and I have a chance to score big ..." I can hear the excitement in his voice, and I try to remember him being this enthusiastic when he worked at his Scarborough office. I can't. Not in the last few years, anyway. I swallow thickly in our bright yellow kitchen, wondering if something good could have come from this move after all.

"... see it as a real growth opportunity for the company. And maybe a sizeable bonus for us," he finishes.

"That's great, Dad. It's just —" I catch myself.

"What, Randy?"

"I wanted to tell you —" I blink again.

"Tell me what, Randy?"

I think about all the whining I've been doing, the constant complaining and finding fault, never once considering how hard it's been for *him* to start all over again. He tried to tell me, but I wouldn't listen. We started all over once before, Dad and I. A sudden parade of memories fills my head, beginning with our first Christmas without my mother, the mantel holding two stockings instead of three. The last memory, of course, is me shouting at him in this kitchen almost a week ago: *"Let's face it, Dad, you don't know anything!"* I guess the person who didn't know anything wasn't my father.

"Randy?"

"I miss you, Dad." And then I'm humiliating myself in front of Norma, making this ridiculous sound that I try to disguise by coughing. She turns away, pretends to straighten cups or something, and I'm grateful for that.

"I miss you, too, Randy." He doesn't need to say it. But it feels good hearing it.

In the background I hear someone call his name. "Look, Randy, there are some people waiting for me. I have to go. You sure you're okay?"

"I'm okay," I manage to say.

"I'll be home tomorrow sometime. See you then, all right?"

"All right, Dad. See you."

I hang up the phone and wipe my eyes with the back of my hand. When I look up, Norma is watching me. And this time she doesn't look away. "Randy," she says, "what's the matter?"

I breathe deeply. I'm about to say *Nothing. Mind your own business.* But another memory floats to the surface — the mantel last Christmas when there were three stockings again. I was furious when I saw it, resentment like a hot coal in my chest that entire holiday. Now, for the first time, I think of the way Dad hung them there — his in the center and Norma's and mine on either side. Why did I always think of hers as being in the middle, separating Dad's from mine?

I don't know what to say to her.

"Somethin's wrong, Randy," she says. Her voice is tentative, softly probing. "I know you think I'm stupid, but you haven't been actin' right for days. I thought you were still upset about the Internet thing, and you prob'ly are. But there's somethin' *else*, isn't there?"

Suddenly I feel like I did Tuesday night, standing outside my body watching myself about to empty that bucket all over Hensford's door. I'm outside myself again now, but this time I'm watching me standing in front of Norma, my hand still on the phone. I'm not holding a bucket, but I have lots of stuff to throw at her. None of it smells, but it's just as messy, just as ugly. It's a whole load of jealousy and distrust that has festered until it's infected everything I've said and done in the last twelve months.

I see myself looking at Norma, the woman whose greatest crime was to meet, love, and marry my father. I see Norma looking at me, her head lowered, her shoulders hunched slightly as she waits for the crap she expects me to throw at her. Norma, who dropped out of school at sixteen, who waited tables for minimum wage plus tips for the next half of her life, and who was waiting tables last October at the Brown Barrel where my father's co-workers surprised him with a birthday party. He told me later that she had the kindest face of anyone he had ever met. It's only now that I'm able to see what he saw.

I look at my feet. "There *is* something wrong, Norma." I swallow hard. "And I don't know what to do about it."

I sit down. She pulls up a chair beside me and sits down, too. She waits. She lets me talk.

There are times I know she'd have liked to stop me, to comment or to ask a question, but she doesn't. I don't plan to tell her everything. Just what happened Tuesday night and then today, with Jake. But after I get started, I find myself reaching back so she'll understand how it all began. Because I need to understand it, too.

In the end, she knows everything. And she knows what I have to do. She doesn't say it, though. She doesn't need to. Because *I* know what I have to do, too.

Chapter 21

"I'm glad you could see us," Norma says as Mr. Hensford opens the door and ushers us in. "I know it's late."

I glance at my watch — 8:55. It took us longer at the police station than I thought it would, and I was ready to call it a night after that. Norma disagreed. "Let's get it all done," she'd said.

And here we are. Getting it done.

"No problem," Hensford says as he directs us to a sofa and then sits in a chair opposite us. Besides a television in the corner, these are the only pieces of furniture in the room. There isn't even a coffee table or a picture on the wall. His ex-wife must have gotten almost everything.

"Now," he says, "perhaps you'd care to tell me what this is all about." I can see in his eyes, though, that he knows. Or thinks he knows.

"My son has something he has to tell you."

I look at her, surprised. She turns to me and smiles encouragingly. There's no trace of the lowered head and hunched shoulders I'm so used to seeing. She looks the way she did the day she started cleaning the house. That was a job that needed doing, too.

I turn to Hensford. "I was one of the people who threw the cow manure on your house," I say.

He nods. I wait for him to say something, but he doesn't.

"I'm very sorry," I say. "I intend to pay for any damage we did. And any expense it might have cost you to clean it up."

He nods.

I look at Norma, but she just smiles at me again.

"I know it was a stupid thing to do," I continue, wanting desperately to fill up the silence in that room.

"Yes," Hensford says, "it was."

"And it'll never happen again."

"No," Hensford murmurs, "I don't expect it will." But it's like he's talking to himself.

Then Norma speaks. "Randy is a good boy, Mr. Hensford. A young man, really. Young men make mistakes. If there's any good to come a' this —"

But Hensford interrupts her. "Who else was involved?"

I'd had a tough time with that question at the police station, although Norma had prepared me for it. I'd just wanted to confess *my* part in the treatment. Ratting on the others, Steve especially, would earn me some interesting attention — considerably more, I knew, than Jerry Lawson got for sitting in Steve's seat at the Regent. But just giving myself up, Norma said, wouldn't be getting the job done. And, somehow, I knew she was right. So I'd told the police what they wanted to know, even though I made sure to add that it wouldn't have happened if I hadn't given the go-ahead. I do the same for Mr. Hensford now.

He nods.

Somewhere outside a dog barks, probably the same one that barked Monday night. A car goes by, and I realize the dog heard it coming before I did. So much seems to have been coming that I didn't know about. Is this the story of my life — never knowing what's coming? A part of me wonders where my mother is, wonders if she thinks about me, if she knows just how deep her roots went as they pressed and pushed against the things that held her in. Probably not. It doesn't matter now, anyway.

Norma stands up. So do I.

"We won't take up any more a' your time," she says. "We just wanted you t'hear it from us. Randy knows he's responsible for what he did. If you'd like to talk to his father about it, he'll be home tomorrow. He's away on business right now."

Hensford shakes his head. "That won't be necessary," he says. "I appreciate your coming here. The back and two sides of the house have to be repainted. I'll send you and the other boys' families a copy of the bill when it's finished. I expect you'll share the cost equally."

"That's fair, Mr. Hensford." Norma extends her hand. "Nice t'meet you." She smiles and I see she's got the sardonic thing down pat. "It woulda been nicer, though, if we'd met under different circumstances."

Hensford smiles slightly, too. "Yes, it would."

We move toward the door, but Hensford stops us. "Randy," he says, and I turn, expecting to see the mocking smile I've been waiting for. But his face looks empty, like something that's been used up. "I know why you did it," he says quietly.

I don't know what to say. I'm not even sure what he means.

"I think I owe you an apology. For the things I said to you in class."

My eyes widen.

He continues. "There are reasons why we do things we shouldn't. Like the manure thing. Reasons don't excuse it, but they help us understand." He pauses, glancing around him at the bare walls. "My wife left me last year. You probably know that."

It's my turn to nod.

"I'm surprised she stayed as long as she did. I'm not an easy person to live with."

I'm tempted to tell him how little *that* surprises me, but I wait for him to continue.

"I've been very angry for a long time." He runs a hand through his hair. "Bitter is probably a better word. Anyway, I've just been going through the motions at school." He looks at me and a sad smile plays at the corners of his mouth. "But you know that, don't you? You know a lot of things. You're very smart, Randy. You did very well at your last school."

I don't know whether this is a statement or a question. I nod again.

"I checked your file. Eaton Academy." He pauses for a moment. Then, "You must think I'm pretty pathetic."

I don't know whether to agree or keep my mouth shut. I keep my mouth shut.

"When you corrected me that day in school, I *felt* pathetic. And I reacted the same way I did with my wife the four years we were married. Lashed out." He looks down at his feet. "I'm sorry, Randy."

I glance at Norma. Her face has the same expression on it she was wearing when I got off the phone with Dad. She nods her head toward the teacher.

"Thanks, Mr. Hensford." I don't know what else to say.

"We'd better be goin'," Norma says.

"There's one thing I'd like to know before you go, Randy," Hensford remarks as Norma opens the door.

"Yes, sir?"

"Why did you tell me you were involved in this? Jake Varner didn't identify you. I don't think he *would* have, either. He's a hard case, that one."

I look at Norma, then at the teacher. "I'd rather not say, Mr. Hensford."

Hensford nods. "All right. I'm glad you came forward, though. That took a lot of courage."

"Thanks," I say. But he's wrong. This was the easy part. I'll need a whole lot more than courage when Jake and the others find out what I've done.

* * * * * *

An alarm is ringing in my head. Two long tones. Silence. Two more long tones. It takes another pair of tones for me to realize it's the phone. I roll over, hearing footsteps padding down the stairway, and I check the glowing numbers on my clock radio — 2:17. I should be asking myself who'd be calling at this time of night, but all my sleep-drugged brain can wonder is if Dad remembered to buy the two extension phones he said he'd pick up at the Price Club in Halifax.

The sound stops in mid-tone and I hear Norma's voice drift up from the kitchen. I can't make out what she's saying, but I hear her voice rise. She's angry. I get up and go out into the hall in time to hear her slam down the phone.

She pads down the hallway to the foot of the stairs just as the phone starts to ring again. She scowls, then looks up and sees me. "It's no-one," she says. "Forget it."

The phone rings and rings and I start down the stairs. "It's for me, isn't it?"

"Forget it," she says, looking up at me. "Just let it ring."

"What about the neighbors?" I ask.

She raises her eyebrows and I can tell she's forgotten about the party line. "I'll take it off the hook," she says, turning around.

"No. I'll do it," I tell her.

"Randy —" she begins, but I brush by her.

In the kitchen I reach for the phone, but my hand freezes over the receiver. Two more rings before I can force myself to pick it up. I don't bother to say hello.

"Is he there?" The male voice on the other end is unrecognizable at first, but not because of any attempt to disguise it. The words are muddy with rage, vowels and consonants a turbid jangle of sounds. "You there, Randy?"

Behind me I hear Norma come into the kitchen. I look at her and she shakes her head, but I shake mine in return. "I'm here, Steve," I say quietly.

The words that fly from the receiver remind

me of the closet where Jerry and I huddled together in the darkness. This time, though, I don't press my fists against my ears. Steve's fury seems to feed on itself with each new epithet.

I see Norma can hear what he's saying, too, and she comes and stands beside me, her hand on my shoulder as we listen together.

"...'n if you think you can pull somethin' like this 'n get away with it, you ain't half as smart as I thought you were." He pauses. "You still there, slime-ball?"

"I'm still here."

There is a long silence. Then, "You're gonna wish you'd never set foot in Brookdale. Matter a' fact, you're gonna wish you'd never been *born*."

Then the click.

I hang up as Norma moves across the kitchen. "What are you doing?" I ask as she pulls down the phone book from one of the shelves over the counter. It seems like a million years ago that she painted them white.

She fans the pages without looking up. "Calling the police."

I go to her and rest my hand on the pages. "Don't."

She looks at me, surprised. "Randy, that boy threatened you. The police —"

"What can they do? They aren't bodyguards. They'll just make it worse."

"But —"

"Look, Norma, I have to handle this myself. It's part of getting the job done. You know?"

"Randy, that boy sounded dangerous."

I try to smile. "He *is* dangerous."

"All the more reason to call —"

I shake my head. "No, Norma. The police can't help me. If I don't take care of this myself, it'll always be there." I think of Bobby Hancock whimpering under Steve's grip that first day in the washroom, of Bobby Hancock eating lunch alone in the cafeteria, of Bobby Hancock hiding out in the computer lab at noon. I shake my head again. "I got myself into this. I have to get myself out."

She looks down at the phone book for a moment. When she looks up again, her face is lined with worry. "What will you do?"

I glance out the window into the darkness. Although I can't see them, I know the waves are out there, rolling over and over as they race toward the shore. I shake my head. "I don't know."

"I wish your father was here," she says quietly.

"So do I." I turn to her. "Norma?"

"Yes, Randy?"

I don't know how to say it so it doesn't sound corny. But I guess words aren't that important after all. It's what's inside them that matters. "I'm glad *you're* here."

She turns away and I see her brush her fingers quickly over her eyes. She clears her throat.

"Since we're up, you want somethin' to eat?" she asks, her voice louder than necessary.

Eating is the absolute last thing I want to do. But I know sleep isn't going to come again for awhile — if at all — and I can tell Norma needs to be doing something. Anything. "Yes," I reply.

Besides, don't condemned men eat one last hearty meal?

Chapter 22

"You're sure you don't want me to go in with you?" she asks.

I remember when she asked me that question a month ago. But the answer I want to give now is different from the one I gave then. A part of me — the part that clung to Dad in a crowded mall so long ago — wants to say *Yes, please come.* But I can't. I shouldn't even have allowed her to drive me to school today, but she wouldn't take no for an answer. She thought it would be better if I arrived late. I just have to get through this one day and then the weekend's here. It would be such a small thing to do if 3:30 weren't light-years away.

"No, Norma. But thanks." I climb out of the car and shut the door.

She leans over so she's looking up through the

passenger window. "Randy?"

"Yes?"

"I packed you somethin' special for lunch."

"Thanks, Norma," I say. "For everything."

She smiles, then her face disappears and the Lumina pulls away from the curb.

I take a deep breath and turn toward the school. Over the outdoor speaker I hear *Would electrostat chloroform acropolis over rubber boots?* Translation: *Would Mrs. Pratt please inform the office of her whereabouts?* My greatest accomplishment in the last month has been learning to decipher Mrs. Belcher's Office-Speak. That and flushing my life down the toilet.

I'm halfway across the yard when I realize something else, something important: I'm not concentrating on walking. Or breathing, for that matter. And I'm not stumbling over my feet or panting like a dog. I'm still marveling over this when I hear it: "*Forsythe!*"

I stop. There's no point in going further.

Jake, Steve, Phil, and Kyle saunter across the lawn from the direction of the parking lot. They've been waiting for me. I adjust my backpack on my shoulder. There's really nothing else I can do. For a second I wish I'd got Norma to drop me at the front entrance. But that wouldn't have changed anything. Delayed it, maybe. But not changed it.

"So. Randy."

"So. Jake." It all sounds so rehearsed. Like a

dance. I take a deep breath.

"You freakin' snitch," Steve murmurs.

"Why'd you do it?" Phil asks, his voice even and quiet. I'm surprised they're speaking so softly. I expected them to be ranting at me by now. It's unnerving. And then I realize that's why they're doing it.

I look at Kyle, who has said nothing. He looks away.

"Jake knows why," I tell them. "Ask *him*."

"You're stupid, Randy," Jake says. "That wouldn't a' been a problem."

"Not for you maybe."

"Your old man prob'ly has more samples lyin' around than he knows what to do with. He wouldn't a' missed a few from time to time."

"Maybe. Maybe not. But I've never stolen anything from my father, Jake. And I wasn't about to start stealing drugs just so Hensford wouldn't find out who did his house."

"But why'd you rat on the rest of us?" Phil asks. His voice is louder now and suddenly I'm aware of people watching us. Not a lot. Four or five. But they know something's up. They see it in the way Jake and the others are standing in front of me. Like predators about to spring.

I look at Phil. "Because what I did was wrong. What *we* did was wrong. I wasn't going to make it worse by lying for you."

"You freakin' snitch," Steve says again, but

this time he's not murmuring.

I hear someone behind me call "Fight!" and then the sound of feet, lots of them, running across the parking lot toward us. In a moment, we're the center of a circle of people, all craning their necks to see.

"Look, I'm sorry. I know that probably doesn't make any difference to you —"

"You're goddam right!" Steve yells at me. "It don't make no difference at all! But that ain't the only thing you're gonna be sorry about."

Comments ripple through the crowd around us, things like "*Give* it to him!" and "Kick his butt!" I don't even recognize the voices saying these things. They're just voices, like fins in black water, circling blood.

Suddenly I feel as though I'm standing at the bottom of a large funnel. It's like everything I've ever done in my whole life has led me here to this place, this moment. Only once have I felt more alone.

I let my backpack slide off my shoulder and down my arm. It hits the ground with a thud and I hear the crowd breathe in as one body. "Let 'im *have* it!" someone shouts.

And they do.

I get in a few punches of my own, my knuckles splitting against someone's teeth, but in seconds I'm on the ground with Steve on top of me. His fists come at me again and again, first my jaw and then every other part of my face, and then he's up and Jake is standing over me, cursing, kicking me in the side. I have never known pain like this. It's like every nerve from my waist to my eyebrows is plugged into an electrical outlet, raw voltage coursing through me as it scrambles my head and my guts, looking for a way out. *I'm* looking for a way out, too.

Frantically, I twist and grab Jake's foot, and he trips, going down with a roar. Amid shouts and jeers, I stagger to my feet only to go down again under Phil's fists as Steve's right knee connects squarely with my groin. That ends it for me, my face pressed into the bloody dirt as I curl and roll in agony. But still the crowd shouts, taunting us, begging for more and more and more.

And then they're silent, melting away like wraiths.

"What's going on here?" a voice barks. Even in the red haze of my pain I wonder what idiot would make a comment like that. Then I see. George Baxter, the vice-principal. Behind him is Mr. Connor and another man, a senior high teacher whose name I don't know. Baxter steps between me and the others while Connor and the senior teacher help me get up. I can't fully straighten, the pain in my side and groin too vivid, but I brush aside their hands so they let me stand alone. I deserve that much.

"The four of you come with me right now!"

Baxter commands.

Four? I turn toward the others and am surprised to see Kyle isn't among them.

Baxter leads us toward the school. As we follow, I see blood streaming from Jake's mouth and Steve's nose. Even though it hurts, I smile.

* * * * * *

". . . and all four of you get five days' suspension. That's board policy for fighting on school grounds. Understand?" Baxter rasps.

As terrible as I feel, I find myself wondering if the school board simply prefers that students do their fighting elsewhere, that this is more a problem of location than anything else. I think of those four-million-dollar renovations that resulted in a music room on the first floor that you have to go upstairs to get to, and I'm not surprised that the board's policy on fighting doesn't make sense. But I nod my head for Baxter anyway, wincing as a white-hot spasm razors from my neck to my jaw.

"You four are already in enough trouble. I got a call from the police last night. I can't understand why you'd want to make it worse by doing something like this."

Why I'd *want* to. Right. Like I woke up today thinking *Now, how can I possibly get myself pulverized before nine o'clock this morning?* Is this guy brain-dead or just naturally stupid?

230

None of us says anything. The vice-prin stares at us another moment, then tells us to wait in the outer office, where right at that moment Mrs. Belcher is calling our parents to come pick us up.

I feel sorry for Norma. She probably hasn't even got home yet. We get up and move toward the doorway. Phil and I get there first. Surprisingly, he steps aside and lets me go ahead.

We have the pleasure of sitting right across from Mrs. Belcher, whose contempt for us manifests itself in a searing glare. Her phone manner is no more pleasant than her face-to-face demeanor: each time she reaches a parent or an answering machine, she delivers the same message laced with disdain: "This is Eileen Belcher calling from the school. Your son was involved in a fight this morning and has been suspended for five days. Please come get him." Short and sweet. You have to admire the intensity of her conviction that none of us is worth the time she's forced to spend on us.

* * * * * *

"Lots of cuts and bruises, and he'll be sore as the devil tomorrow, but nothing's broken," the doctor says. His voice sounds enormous in this tiny room. "He might like to see a dentist about that chipped tooth, though."

Norma, who wouldn't take me home without stopping at Brookdale Hospital's outpatients department, exhales. It's like she's been holding her breath the entire time the doctor's been poking and probing me. "You're sure?" she asks.

He nods. "I'd recommend ice packs, especially for his nose and forehead, and the maximum dosage of acetaminophen for the next couple of days. Other than that, he just needs lots of rest. And fluids, too."

I don't know what makes doctors think anyone under the age of twenty is incapable of understanding the spoken word. They always talk to the nearest adult. If Norma weren't standing here, he'd probably be speaking to the cleaning lady who came in a moment ago to empty the wastebasket. I could care less, though — the upside is that I don't need X rays. I'd hate to have to see Mrs. Varner right now.

"Thanks, doctor," Norma says. She helps me slip on my jacket and I ease myself off the examining table.

"Thanks," I add, but he's already out the door.

The walk to the Lumina takes longer than I would have thought possible, and the trip home is an exercise in trying not to let any part of my body touch the seat for more than a few seconds. By the time we roll up the driveway, I'm actually glad to see the bay. Norma helps me into the house and runs a bath for me in the mauve tub, then tries again to call my father.

It takes me five minutes to undress and almost

as long to get into the tub. I wince as the soap stings the cuts on my hands and arms, and for a moment I don't think I'll be able to convince my body to unbend and stretch out. But finally it does. I lie there until the water starts to get cool, then I run some more hot and lie back again. I have every intention of spending the rest of my life in this tub.

* * * * * *

"And you're *sure* you're all right?"

"Yes, Dad. I'm fine." I yawn sleepily and my jaw cracks in two. Or feels like it, anyway.

He looks like he's going to start pacing again, and my head can't stand the sound of his shoes on the hard floor. I tell him to sit down.

He could have sat in the chair by my desk, but he doesn't, choosing instead to sit on the bed beside me. He reaches out and puts the back of his hand on my forehead, the way he used to when I was small and had the flu or measles or any of a dozen other bugs that kept him by my bed all hours of the day and night. I wonder now where he got the strength to do it all alone. At the time, it never occurred to me that he could get tired. Or sick, too. He was just there. Always just there.

"You don't have a fever," he says.

"I'm fine, Dad. Really." I feel another yawn

coming on, but I suppress it.

I can tell he doesn't believe me, but he doesn't force the issue. "Norma said you had a couple calls while you were sleeping. One was the girl from the motel."

"Colleen."

"Right. She wanted to know how you were. Norma told her and said you'd call her back when you're feeling better."

"I will." There's a lot I want to tell her. Mostly about what an ass I've been.

"The other was from a girl, too, but she didn't leave her name."

Natalie. I wonder what she might have said to me. For a smart girl, she has a lot to learn. But then, so did I. And there's no prize for learning the hard way like I did. "Maybe she'll call again," I say. And maybe she won't. But I figure if she does, she might be ready to listen.

"Right," my dad says. Then he shakes his head. "I don't understand how all this could happen."

"I'm sorry, Dad." It seems like such a dumb thing to say, but I mean it.

"You'd *better* be," he says raggedly, but I can tell by his nostrils that he's more relieved than upset. No flaring.

He looks at me for a long moment until I almost ask what he's thinking about. Hensford's house? The fight? Our argument last weekend? I want things to be okay between us again.

"Norma told me some other things, too," he says softly.

Oh. "I've been a real jerk, Dad. I know that now. Norma's been great. I wouldn't have been able to get through this without her."

He tries to make a joke of it. "You call this getting *through* it? I'd hate to think what you'd look like if you'd stopped halfway." But then he lowers his head and he's speaking to his hands, folded on his lap. "Look, Randy, I never meant for you to think you weren't important in my life."

"Dad, it's okay —"

"No, it's not. Hear me out. I know the last year has been hard on you, Randy. My meeting Norma and getting married. The restructuring at Healthaid and the months of uncertainty about my job. Then having to move down here, leaving your school, your friends. I guess I was pretty stupid to think I could keep everything together, make everything fit the way I wanted it to. So much has happened so fast. And now here you are in trouble with the law and fighting at school ..." His voice trails off and he gets up and stands by the window, looking out. It's almost dark outside. I must have slept longer than I thought.

He takes a deep breath before continuing. "I called Fish's parents after I finished talking with Norma. They said their offer still stands. You can live with them while you go to Eaton. I'll find the money somewhere."

I'm not sure I've heard him right. His back to me, he seems to be speaking from somewhere far away. "I can go back to Eaton?"

He turns, but he doesn't look at me. He speaks softly, staring at a spot just over my head. "I'll have to get confirmation from the registrar first, though. I'm not sure what their policy is on accepting students with the school year already underway. And this stuff in Brookdale won't help." He takes another deep breath. "But your previous record at Eaton and the work you did on that office program should count in your favor. They know you're a good student."

I just look at him. After all this, I can't believe it. I can go back to Eaton.

He moves over to the bed, reaches down and brushes the hair away from my eyes. He hasn't done that since I was in elementary school. And I'm not sure he knows he's done it now. Like his voice at the window, his eyes seem far away, too. "It's the best thing. I see that now." Then he straightens. "Look, you get some more rest. We'll talk about this tomorrow. Do you need anything else? Some soup? A drink?"

I shake my head slowly. I can go back to Eaton.

"You call us if you need anything."

"Okay," I say.

And then I'm on those gray waves that lift and rock me, carrying me toward the shore and beyond.

Chapter 23

I can go back to Eaton.

I'm standing in Colleen's garden. The fountain is working, but all I hear is the soft hum of the pump beneath it. There is no splash, no rhythmic measure of water returning to water. I look above my head and see a fluid column shooting straight into the air, up and up and up. I think briefly of the plant in *Jack and the Beanstalk* reaching higher and higher into the clouds. Then I imagine Jack standing with an axe above the fallen stalk, smugly victorious. But he doesn't see the roots that stretch deep into the ground, green tendrils parting soil, slicing earth, crumbling clay.

The fountain becomes a faucet and I'm standing in a crowded washroom watching Bobby Hancock dig deep in the pocket of his jeans. He's searching for something, reaching down and down and down, his arm a vertical column of flesh moving endlessly earthward. Someone says, "Looks like this is your lucky day, Bobby," as his arm keeps going. But it's no longer an arm. It's a root the color of emeralds extending beneath Bobby's pant leg, punching its way through the gray tile floor into airless space beneath.

I'm standing on tile floor, but it's white and smooth and it stretches in all directions as far as I can see. There's a dandelion growing up through a jagged crack in this sterile landscape, its stem an exclamation point for its existence. Its yellow head bobs a finger's length above the cool white surface, but its roots stretch down forever.

I can go back to Eaton.

The words repeat themselves like a mantra over and over again while the earth opens in long, brown wounds.

* * * * * *

My head is going to explode. The phone is ringing, but it feels like it's inside my skull. If the sound is that loud up here, it must be blowing a wall out of the kitchen below me. I open my eyes and there on my desk is a sleek new extension phone with dozens of buttons. Dad remembered to stop at the Price Club after all.

I roll over and then catch my breath as every

muscle in my body screams, *Hey, Randy! Remember us?* I'm suddenly willing to let the phone ring itself to death, but the sound is piercing. No, shattering is more accurate. After plugging it in, Dad must have tried switching off the ringer but turned up the volume instead.

The person on the other end of the line is persistent and, since no-one appears to be answering any other phone in the house, I drag myself up off the bed and over to my desk. "Hello?"

"Randy! You okay?" I recognize Bobby Hancock's voice. Over the phone, he sounds even smaller than he looks.

"Hi, Bobby. Yeah, I'm okay."

"I saw the fight yesterday. From upstairs in Mrs. Lloyd's room. By the time I got outside, Baxter was there."

"I don't think it qualifies as a fight, Bobby. It couldn't have lasted more than a minute and a half, although it seemed like twenty from where I was standing." I correct myself. "I mean, from where I was lying down."

I don't expect a big laugh, but he could at least chuckle politely. Instead, he says, "I don't know how you did it, Randy."

"Well, basically I just made contact between my back and the ground."

Still nothing. I don't think I've played a tougher audience. "What's wrong, Randy?" he asks after a moment.

"I hurt everywhere except my toenails, and they're putting me on notice as we speak."

"Not that. You sound," he gropes for a word, "indifferent. Like none of this matters."

"Oh, it matters all right. I'm sure Jake and his buddies aren't finished with me yet."

"I think you're wrong about that."

"And what makes you so sure?"

"Didn't you *hear* everyone?" he asks.

"Who? When?"

"The crowd. The people standing around you."

I frown and my face reminds me that it takes fewer muscles to smile. "Oh. The ones who were telling Jake and Steve and Phil and Kyle how to obliterate me."

"Kyle left," he says. "He never laid a finger on you. And that *isn't* what the others were saying. Not everybody."

I'm tempted to frown again, but I don't. "Look, Bobby, I was there. I know what that crowd was saying. I heard them."

"Not everyone was cheering for *them*. Lots of people were cheering for *you*. And afterward, you should have heard the talk. About how you actually turned Steve and Phil in to the cops, how you didn't back down in the schoolyard even though you were outnumbered. That took real guts. Jake and Steve and the rest lost something yesterday. Credibility. I think they're going to leave you alone."

I look at the phone, surprised by everything Bobby has told me. So getting the crap kicked out of me in front of half the school wasn't a total waste of a morning after all. I shake my head. "It doesn't matter anyway, Bobby. I'm not staying."

"What do you mean?"

"I'm going back to Eaton. If my father can arrange it."

There's silence for a moment, except for the faint hiss of the phone line. Then, "When?"

"I don't know yet. Soon, I hope."

"Oh." Like a single drop of water from a tap.

Outside I hear a car start, then a door open below me as someone comes into the kitchen. "Look, Bobby, I have to go. Talk to you later, all right? Before I leave."

"Randy?"

"Yes?"

Another silence. A long one.

"You still there, Bobby?" I ask.

"Thanks for being my friend, Randy." He says it quickly like it's one long word instead of six. Then he hangs up.

I'm still looking at the receiver in my hand as Dad comes up the stairs carrying a suitcase. "You're awake," he says. "How're you feeling?"

"Sore," I say, "but I'll live."

He grins. "That's good because you owe me money. Your teacher, Mr. Hensford, was just here. Norma and I were outside talking with him. He got an estimate for the paint job and dropped by a copy. You'll be pleased to know he's decided not to press charges. He said that getting things cleaned up is more important." He puts the suitcase on the bed. "Funny, though."

"What's funny?"

"I know he was talking about the paint on his house, but I got the impression he meant something else." Dad shrugs. "Anyway, good news, bad news. You're now square with Mr. Hensford and the police, but the bill I paid today comes out of your allowance."

I groan. "When will I be paid up?"

"Let's just say you won't be making any major purchases for quite a while."

I shake my head, then look at the suitcase. "Something up?"

"More good news. I talked with the registrar, which, let me tell you, wasn't easy on a Saturday. He agreed to a conditional acceptance to be reviewed at the end of November."

"Really?" I can't believe it.

"You start on Monday. I've been on the phone all morning. Fish's parents are expecting you tomorrow."

"What about the money?"

"I called Healthaid's regional director, Ray Wallis, this morning. I was right about getting a bonus. It'll take care of your tuition until the November review. We'll worry about the rest when the time comes. We'll manage somehow." He unzips the suitcase and opens it, all the time talking fast as though he'll forget something if he doesn't say it all at once. "I made reservations for you with Air Canada. We have to leave by six tomorrow morning to get to the airport on time for your flight, so you'll have to get everything packed up and ready to go tonight. You can only take one suitcase and a carry-on, so we'll have to send most of your stuff on after you. You'd better pick out the clothes you'll want to wear for the next week or so." He moves toward the door. "Lots to do, so don't be long."

I can go back to Eaton.

"Dad?"

"Hmm?" he asks from the doorway. He's looking at something out in the hall.

"You're okay with this?"

"I just want what's best for you, Randy." And then he's gone.

* * * * * *

"You been down here quite a while," Norma says.

"Just watching the sun set."

She kneels down beside me on the grass. "It's beautiful," she says.

And it is. I've never seen the bay this still. It's like glass all the way to New Brunswick. And the air is so clear you'd swear you can see buildings over there instead of just a vague outline of land against sky. It's the ugly duckling thing all over again — who'd have thought there was a swan beneath all that gray turbulence?

Actually, as beautiful as this is, I miss the gray. I've grown used to the dark rhythm of the Fundy shoreline: the rise and fall of the tides, the endless roll of the waves, the constant pounding of the surf on the rocks below this cliff. The scene before us now seems almost like a VCR on pause. Or a candle with no flame.

"It's like there's somethin' missin', though," Norma says.

I look at her, surprised. "I was just thinking the same thing."

She turns to me and smiles. I smile, too.

We look out over the water a while longer. There are waves in my head made of words, things I want to say that won't come together. About how I misjudged her, how I'm sorry for the things I've said, the things I've done. Just when I think I know what it is I want to tell her, the words roll and toss, shattering themselves like the spray I'm used to seeing below me. I take a deep breath. "Norma, I'm really sorry —"

But she cuts me off. "I know it's been rough sharin' your father with me. You had him all to yourself for so many years. I don't blame you for not wantin' that to change. I'd have felt the same way if things had been reversed."

It's good to hear her say this, but I know it isn't true. I start to tell her that, but she hasn't finished. "I don't want you to go, Randy."

My face must register my astonishment. How can she say that after everything I've done, all the times I've torn her down? *She's* the brave one. I see that now.

She looks out across the water. "Your father loves you very much, Randy. You know that."

"I know that," I say quietly.

She turns to me. "You goin' is tearin' him apart."

I think of all the arrangements he's taken care of, the calls he's made. "He hasn't said anything."

"He wouldn't. That's why he's up there now," she says, nodding toward the house behind us. "He doesn't know I'm tellin' you this."

"Then why —"

"He thinks goin' is what you want."

I turn and see the end of the verandah that still isn't finished. "You don't think it is?"

"You two've been a fam'ly for a long time."

I wonder if he'll finish shingling it by himself. *It's a lot easier to tear something down than it is to rebuild it.* "Yes, we have," I tell her.

"What *do* you want, Randy?"

What do I want? It's been so long since any-one's asked me that question I don't know what to say. What *do* I want? To return to Eaton, of course. To be with my friends. To make everything the same as it was before.

Except there's a problem. Without Dad, nothing *could* be the same.

To my left, three gnarled trees slant toward the east, away from the setting sun and the wind that, for once, is not blowing. The roots of one of the trees are already exposed on one side, the soil around them having washed into the sea below. I think about those trees clinging here to the top of this cliff. Every element seems against them — rain, wind, ice, snow — yet still they stand, their roots anchored deep beneath them. What was it Dad said the first time he brought us to Lewis Cove? *"Here's a chance for us to build some permanence into our lives, put down some solid roots."* For the first time, I realize it was those roots that I've been afraid of all this time. Roots that would push and press against the things that hold them in, cracking them, crumbling them, tearing them apart.

But roots don't *have* to tear people apart. I know that now.

I look at Norma. *"This* is what I want," I say.

She smiles again. "I know."

We sit there together till it's nearly dark. Then we go back to the house and my father.

THE END